NIGHT OF THE SHORT EYES

NIGHT OF THE SHORT EYES

a novel

PETER PLATE

SEVEN STORIES PRESS
New York • Oakland • London

Copyright © 2023 by Peter Plate

SEVEN STORIES PRESS www.sevenstories.com

Library of Congress Cataloging-in-Publication Data

Names: Plate, Peter, author.
Title: Night of the short eyes / Peter Plate.
Description: New York, NY : Seven Stories Press, [2023]
Identifiers: LCCN 2023000854 | ISBN 9781644213148 (paperback) | ISBN
    9781644213155 (electronic)
Subjects: LCGFT: Noir fiction. | Novels.
Classification: LCC PS3566.L267 N54 2023 | DDC 813/.54--dc23/eng/20230109
LC record available at https://lccn.loc.gov/2023000854

College professors and high school and middle school teachers may order free examination copies of Seven Stories Press titles. Visit https://www.sevenstories. com/pg/resources-academics or email academics@sevenstories.com.

Printed in the USA.

9 8 7 6 5 4 3 2 1

For

Jimmy and Donald, Curt and Robert,
Dennis, Kathi, and Ricky

You are a tiger, you are a lion, you are a cat.

—ISAAC BABEL

PART ONE

SOUTH OF MARKET

ONE

The badlands. That's what a voice in my head said when mom walked into the kitchenette wearing nothing but an unbuttoned men's dress shirt, her bush bigger than the moon as she glided to the sink—dad leaned on the counter next to his partner Ronnie, a gun thief like himself. The floor was strewn with stolen rifles. It was the first night of summer.

Two days later I was outside a Pacific Heights mini-mansion, a spanking new three-story glass and steel house rumored to have loads of expensive guns. Dad had creepy-crawled into the place through a ground-level bathroom window to see if he could swipe them.

I was the lookout.

I snuck a glance at the street. There were no passing cars, no one was hanging on the sidewalk either. I checked the neighbor's home, another mini-mansion with red and orange bougainvillea scaling its granite walls. Birds yakked in palm trees. A train whistle echoed from the flatlands by Mission Bay. A foghorn boomed somewhere off Point Bonita.

The coast was clear.

I kneeled to retie a shoelace—they never stayed tight enough—while the ocean wind that blew through the Golden Gate Bridge kicked up dust and tickled my nose.

I was going on thirteen—my birthday was in two months. Sixty days. Fourteen hundred and forty hours. And I wanted a cake. A chocolate cake with fudge frosting and a maraschino cherry on top, my name in white vanilla icing. A skyscraper birthday cake, tall and wide.

Lost in my daydream—swimming in it—I didn't notice the two undercover SWAT cops sidling up the driveway. The next thing I knew, I was thrown to the ground—I weighed sixty pounds—and handcuffed. Right then, dad chucked a pillowcase fat with pistols out the bathroom window. He saw the cops haul me away and yowled, "Hey, man! Fucking hell! You can't do this!"

That was seven weeks ago. Dad was sent to the state pen at Muscupiabe yesterday. The second time in five years for gun theft. He blamed me. It was my fault, all my fault. I'd let him down by not doing my job.

If that wasn't enough, Frankie Jones, a girl from around the way, got knocked up by a Crusade for Jesus boy some months ago. Her parents had locked her up inside their apartment—now they were shipping her to Bakersfield to have the baby.

Frankie's long-time neighbor, a seventeen-year-old stickup artist named Superman, flipped over it. "Frankie ain't got nothing. She's the kind of poor that when you're bending over to pick up a penny off the ground, she'll come by and lift the wallet from your pocket. You know what the Crusade boy did to her at that party in Glen Canyon. The motherfucker. Now she's getting exiled to Bakersfield. The pregnant girl diaspora. It ain't right. That's what Superman says."

◻ ◻ ◻

It rained and rained the afternoon Superman cursed the Crusade boy. I walked south of Market, direct from juvie after the bust with dad. I passed sun-bleached Crusade for Jesus pamphlets stacked at a Muni bus stop, and I passed the fortress-like liquor store on Mission Street that got robbed last December—everyone said Superman was behind the heist.

The rain had me thinking hard. I didn't know if Frankie Jones would ever come home. I was sure dad wouldn't. Some people went to prison. Some went to Bakersfield. Then I caught sight of Superman on Natoma—he was styling a pink velvet track suit. He moved fast and talked out loud to himself, and waved his fists like he was stone cold nuts.

I continued to slog through the downpour—until I got a fix on dad a block ahead of me. A classic Thompson submachine gun was carelessly slung over his shoulder. Two bandoliers of dumdum bullets drooped from his neck. I squawked, "Dad, dad!" He wheeled around at the sound of my petulant voice, but it wasn't him—it was my imagination going off the rails. For dad had done what he'd always done, he had done a vanishing act, getting further and further away from me, back to the pen, maybe this time for good.

TWO

The rat-a-tat-tat drumbeat of the rain on our roof scratched at my ears while I slept that night. I dreamed about Frankie Jones—her angelic face bobbed on the ceiling over my cot. I smiled and hugged myself.

I was at the front door when the sun made a comeback in the morning, climbing over the palm treetops as Bob the social worker steered his white county sedan into our oil-stained courtyard driveway. It was an ambush, a surprise visit, not a good sign—you were supposed to go to the welfare office to discuss food stamp applications.

Decked out in a camouflage safari suit, Bob shuffled past me into our one-bedroom garage apartment like he owned the place. He nodded at mom and trudged to the kitchenette, his big feet slapping on the funky linoleum floor. He stopped at the refrigerator, opened the door, and poked his masked, moon-white mug inside it.

Fortunately, there wasn't a thing in the fridge.

Not if you wanted food stamps.

While Bob inspected the refrigerator, mom roosted on the living room couch, and tracked him with gray, knowing eyes. Two bottles of antidepressants were moored at her feet, red and white tablets, Tofranil and Prozac, scattered across the floor no different than semi-precious jewels. She hissed at me: "Your father won't be leaving the penitentiary any time soon. Possibly never. We can only hope. I must consider my prospects. I should remarry. This time, a nice man."

I was silent, the safest place on earth.

Bob finished his investigation and declared, "Your application is good. I'll call you soon."

The social worker departed and mom got on the horn to the old lady—her mother—jabbering in Russian so I wouldn't get what she was saying, her strategy ever since I was a rug rat. That meant it was serious business, probably about dad going to the joint. I left her to it, and stole into the bedroom I shared with my younger brother Putin, nicknamed so on account of his broken English and heavy accent. He squatted by his cot, and drank me in with cool blue eyes while Public Enemy thumped on his tape player. "I'm constructing a bomb," he said matter-of-factly. "It's fucking extraordinary."

Russian was the first language in our household.

Profanity in English was the second tongue.

Everybody called my brother Putin, including me. Except mom never did. It was disrespectful to the Russian leader, whose handsome face, she said dreamily, reminded her of her first husband. A man shot to death by the border patrol while smuggling contraband from Canada into the United States.

Dad was mom's third husband. Or fourth. In advance of his return to Muscupiabe—on a twenty-five-year stretch—he'd intended to call us from the jail at 850 Bryant to say goodbye. The call was canceled because he had to meet with his lawyer to talk about turning state's evidence against Ronnie. Should dad rat on his partner, he'd get a chance to shorten his sentence.

Mom said we'd go upstate to visit dad at Muscupiabe. I couldn't wait.

In the meantime, Putin and I divided our days between the garage apartment and the clinic on Harrison Street. The clinic—a Christian academy headquartered in a one-time industrial laundry facility—was managed by the Crusade for Jesus organization, thanks to a contract with the Division of Juvenile Justice. Everyone from juvie—in the wake of detention—was pipelined to the clinic. Black kids, Cambodians, Mexicans, Pacific

Islanders, and a handful of white boys. Five hundred strong with nothing but talk about Jesus all day long—on a campus that was a dead ringer for a police station.

◻ ◻ ◻

Fresh from juvie, I was processed into the clinic on a foggy afternoon. I was fingerprinted. I had an unflattering digital mug shot taken of me. An electronic bracelet was attached to my right leg. The clinic's instructors then shepherded me to a cubicle—the prayer room—a windowless space with a mural of Jesus painted on the walls. The instructors forced me to kneel on the floor, so that I stared up at Jesus. They told me to pray for absolution. The bust in the Pacific Heights mini-mansion. I didn't beg for Jesus's forgiveness, I would go to purgatory. Even worse, I'd get violated to prison.

The instructors said we had a lifelong relationship with Jesus. They employed chalkboards in their sessions to make diagrams—in white chalk only—about Jesus and us. Diagram after diagram, lots of dotted lines, every one of them leading to Jesus. He was in the driver's seat. We were the passengers.

The scuttlebutt had it that the instructors imprisoned Donny Waters—a pint-sized sixteen-year-old hustler who went by the handle of the Lone Ranger—in the prayer room for two days. They'd grilled him around the clock until he wigged out and got dispatched to the Napa State nuthouse. Yesterday, the Lone Ranger was at a Jesus session. His instructor, an alcoholic white lady known as Frankenstein, called him a homosexual. That was what she said to the Lone Ranger. Because he rode the bus to Oakland on weekends to turn tricks by the Fruitvale BART station. But what did she know about anything? The old lush. It wasn't even true. The Lone Ranger never turned tricks in Oakland. Anyway, sessions at the clinic had been suspended since Frankenstein—she refused to wear a mask on religious grounds—tested positive.

THREE

The night after Bob the social worker came by, heat lightning crackled in the sky near the Golden Gate Bridge and mosquitos clamored at my ears. Frankenstein said I was a KGB agent—she wanted to know when I'd poison her. Everybody at the clinic had been gossiping about Frankie Jones, how the Crusade boy wouldn't claim her child as his—he was now headed to a posh boarding school in New York.

I was in the bedroom fiddling with my electronic ankle bracelet when mom appeared out of nowhere by my cot. She was in a sheer black negligee, her hands were poised in mid-air, her white face oily and unfocused. For an instant, I recognized her for what she once was. Young with unlined skin. Just as quickly, she became old. She melted into the shadows, and retreated from the room to the living room where the radio burbled Prokofiev. It happened so fast, it must've been the dark acting funny.

Putin monitored me from his cot. But I didn't see him. I saw the cops arresting me in the mini-mansion's driveway. I saw dad at the bathroom window, a pillowcase stuffed with guns on the sill. I screamed and screamed until Putin bellowed at me to shut the fuck up.

I put a blanket over my face, and kept screaming.

◻ ◻ ◻

The next morning came too fast. Crows cawed from the roof. Flies slammed into the screen door. Mom brewed instant coffee in the kitchenette, her back to me. Then Bob the social worker telephoned. We had to visit his office, like pronto. Our food stamp application needed tuning.

Off we went to welfare. Putin and I soldiered up Mission Street with mom leading our sorry parade. She was dressed for the excursion in frayed denim short-shorts, her bleached hair fiery white in the gray sunlight. We were at Ninth Street, bickering among ourselves about the social worker, with Putin arguing Bob wanted to get into mom's pants, when a SWAT security patrol stopped us. The officer-in-charge, a pimply white cat in mirrored shades, asked mom for identification. She dismissed him with a scornful glance. "I no need stupid identification. Everybody knows who I am."

The cop mimicked her. "Everybody knows who I am. What bullshit. You're coming down to the station, lady."

Mom grimaced and tugged at her shorts. "What for?"

"You don't have any ID," the cop remarked. "You got a strange accent. C'mon, let's go."

It was wonderful. We weren't going to the welfare office. Mom was going to jail. Smart for him, Putin kept his trap shut—his accent was stronger than anybody's. Mom double-talked the cops out of taking him and me to the clink. "Don't be cruel to my little ones. Their father is in prison. They are sad." The cops bought into her argument—letting us go meant less paperwork for them. Mom ordered Putin and me to return home, which we gladly did.

□ □ □

Shortly before midnight, mom was freed by the fuzz— no charges had been filed against her. She rebounded to the garage apartment cloaked in the aura of martyrdom. A warning for us to keep away from her.

At three in the morning it was still too hot to sleep. The din of the mosquitos was unbearable. I went outside to get some air and came upon Putin bathing in a streetlamp's light by our building—he was flinging rocks at a cat he'd trapped next to a car. I snapped my fingers at him. "Cut the crap."

Putin got ready to heave a rock at me. The mad hatred on his pinched face was breathtaking. "No, I don't want to."

"For fuck's sake, do it."

Reluctantly, he obeyed me, and lowered his arm. A chill ran up my spine—I'd angered Putin. That was not kosher.

Unlike Putin or mom, I had an excellent command of English. No accent. No florid old world gesticulations or mannerisms. Good English defended me against Frankenstein. It protected me from Bob the social worker, and the rest of the world. It was a war of consonants and vowels. My war.

FOUR

Mom had forgotten to take her Prozac and Tofranil cocktail—the excitement with the SWAT cops yesterday. Without it, she zoomed out of control. She accused me of drinking too much milk. I didn't know what she was getting at. The last time I'd looked, there was no milk in the fridge, none for a week. I told her that—I was rewarded with a slap across the chops.

I reeled from the kitchenette to the bedroom.

Putin wasn't there.

A half hour later, I reported to the clinic—it had reopened with upgraded medical guidelines. I raced to the trailer where my Jesus session was scheduled. Back at the helm following a false positive test result, Frankenstein—with no mask—ejected me the second I entered her classroom. She swiveled her powdered face in my direction. "Look at you. What a blasphemer. I don't want you here."

I was speechless. My adopted language—the words I could recite in unaccented, well-modulated English—

was fucking useless. Frankenstein jerked her thumb at the door. I was gone.

Dazed by my expulsion—it would cause a ruckus with juvie—I met up with Putin outside the clinic. He was in the vacant lot across the street sharing a cigarette with Superman.

I said hello to Superman, and listened with one ear while he bad-mouthed the Lone Ranger for his mental health problems. Superman vexed the Lone Ranger had OCD. "The cat has issues." I shrugged my shoulders— everyone I knew had issues. Then Putin and I schlepped south on Mission Street by the Yangtze Market and the Mission Cultural Center to visit the old man—our grandfather—at the orange stucco bungalow he shared with the old lady in the Excelsior neighborhood.

The moment Putin and I stepped into our grandparents' house, we were attacked by cabbage fumes from their kitchen. The old man was stationed in the living room in his rocking chair, modeling a blue wife-beater that showcased his still-powerful chest. He stared out the window at the street.

"What's going on, old man?"

He flicked his Tartar-like eyes at my brother and me, barely registering our presence. He was a million miles away with his memories. Fighting the Nazis as a teen-aged partisan. Hunting them in the snow with a knife. His silences—ninety-five years of them—enveloped the living room.

I had a couple of Bernard Malamud and Isaac Bashevis Singer novels on me—the old man's favorite authors after Pushkin. I handed him the books—he took them with no comment, letting his eyes drift to the window where the memories eagerly awaited him. Enemies in the snow. Partisans with frostbitten feet. The old lady—in a floral-print sack dress—observed us from the kitchen doorway. A wreath of cabbage vapors swirled above her gray head.

The old man had given the old lady his railroad pension, my mother the color of his eyes, keeping for himself only his thoughts, which he didn't share with Putin or me—he never talked to us. Putin and I said adios to him and the old lady, and headed out the door to Mission Street.

The same evening mom careened into the kitchenette in a men's dress shirt—with her bush on display—Ronnie had chauffeured Putin, dad, and me to his home in Berkeley. To get a load of the fawn he'd rescued from a brush fire behind Napa State.

Ronnie directed us to the garage at his house. "Okay, you guys, you gotta be cool." He switched on the light—the fawn was in a baby crib wedged between crates of AK-47 rifles. The young deer quailed at the sight of Putin—its ears twitched in fear while dad and Ronnie fussed over the rifle crates. I nagged Putin. "You make the deer nervous."

He stuck his tongue out at me. "And you're a shitbag."

I was shocked. "I'm a shitbag?"

"Yeah. So go fuck yourself."

The fawn goggled at us.

I wasn't sure how or when Putin would do it, because I didn't know many things about life, like if I'd ever hear a kind word, something I hadn't heard since the world began, but some day Putin would make me pay for nagging him about the deer. For now I sashayed at his side as the surveillance cameras on Mission Street watched us go by. Yes, I moaned to myself. Putin will make you suffer.

Putin grabbed my arm. "Look over there." A fire burned in southern Marin County near Mount Tamalpais, sheets of flame lighted the sky over the San Francisco Bay. A northerly wind pushed the fire's smoke past the Golden Gate into the city while Putin and I slouched by the liquor store Superman took down in December, the month after Frankie Jones became pregnant. The month before the voices in my head—the things I heard that nobody else did—got the better of me.

FIVE

Frankie Jones arrived at the Crusade boys' illegal, secret Glen Canyon cabin on the evening of their party and a kid she'd never seen before twittered, "Hey, hey, Frankie is here." He gave her a beer and she chugged it, spraying foam on her favorite blouse. Christmas lights were strung about the dank cabin, tinkling white boy laughter rose and fell from its unswept corners. Frankie moseyed to a room where some guys were playing cards on a rumpled, unmade bed. She flopped down next to them, just as her boyfriend materialized from thin air, drunker than hell. He asked the other guys to leave. When they cleared out, he nuzzled Frankie's neck, and croaked, "I love you, girl."

Six weeks later, Frankie told her folks she was pregnant, that a Crusade kid was involved. The details were hazy, something to do with a blowout in Glen Canyon. Her father smacked her in the face—her mother caterwauled like the world had ended, instead of having heard the news a baby might get born.

Frankie had blood on her teeth when her father herded her into the side bedroom. "You slut. Don't even think about an abortion. You ain't getting one. It's the devil's work and you're too young for it."

He shut the door, and locked it.

Frankie was sequestered in the bedroom for how long, she didn't know—weeks and weeks. Every day she sat in a chair by the window, the linoleum floor cold under her feet. The sun beat against the window, flies droned at the screen.

The baby in her grew—she began to change.

One afternoon footsteps pitter-pattered in her sun-blasted driveway. They were furtive, cat burglar–like—she didn't know who they belonged to. Then she picked out the Russian kids that lived around the corner on Minna. The older one examined her silhouette in the window. His brother, whiter than a sheet, fell to his knees and clasped his hands together. A couple of seconds went by before Frankie realized he was praying. It took another second to realize he was praying for her.

Somebody had to. Because no angels cooed in her ear. Nobody wanted her any more than the baby's father wanted his child—she'd never felt so alone in her life. All she could do was watch the Russian boy pray in the overheated sunlight.

The night Frankie was deported to Bakersfield she sat in the back seat of her parents' Ford Galaxy with a cardboard suitcase by her side. She contemplated the Bay Bridge, the cities of Berkeley and Oakland, and the Central Valley's treeless landscape as it danced by her window. Mile after mile passed before her eyes. Then, the lights of Bakersfield took shape, becoming brighter and brighter. Before Frankie could fathom what was happening, she got deposited at her aunt and uncle's house, a beige stucco structure on the edge of town.

Her folks cut and ran without saying goodbye to her.

SIX

The smoke from the Marin County fire—burning east of Sausalito to Tiburon—smothered the city and turned the sky brown. The air was unbreathable.

Superman swung by the garage apartment at dusk on Monday. He scoped out our digs and frowned at me. "Superman wants to know how come you ain't got a damn thing in here."

Other than mom's couch, her radio, and our cots, we didn't have a stick of furniture. No chairs or tables. An empty house with little to eat—it was a family tradition.

That's the way it was for the old man and the old lady in Russia during the war. The Nazis appropriated the food and furniture, and razed everything else to the ground. I didn't explain this to Superman—he wouldn't get it.

At Superman's prodding, Putin and I walked with him over to Market Street. There were no cars on the road, no people hitting the pavement, no cops or homeless, and no birds or insects in the smoking brown skyline.

I didn't see or hear a thing, except the Bank of America tower backlit against the plasma-red sun, and the symphony of voices twaddling in my head.

Putin marched in front of us, swaying from side to side with his head held high. Superman swaggered stiff-kneed behind Putin, making like he was in lockup and wanted the cops to know he wasn't scared of them. I plodded after Putin and Superman, flashing to when I was young. How upbeat I was at six and seven. But now I was older—the milestone of becoming thirteen drawing nearer—and I was pissed off. Superman had witnessed Frankie Jones's deportation to Bakersfield; her parents had driven away at nightfall because they didn't want anybody to see them.

Superman whined, "It was a kidnapping, man."

Superman said the mayor stated on television yesterday if there was any civil unrest in the city the police would shoot looters and rioters on sight. This meant Black folks in the Bayview and Mexicans from the Excelsior. Superman's grandfather had told him that during the 1966 riots, Crusade boys gathered on Van Ness Avenue with baseball bats and tire irons—waiting for Black kids to march into the white neighborhoods.

The Crusade boys at the clinic baited Putin about his pidgin English. They called him a Russian spy. Putin shined them on by mingling with the Mexicans. He smoked weed with them in McLaren Park. Attended their parties on Shotwell Street. He went to their parents' houses Sunday mornings for menudo. He'd also picked up Spanglish. Putin's native Russian was capable of inventing made-up words from regular words. Spanglish fit him tighter than a burglar's glove.

Putin faced his enemies—the Crusade boys—with savage exultation. It pleased him that they wanted to kick his ass—he was proud of their dislike for him. He wouldn't have settled for anything less—he would've felt disrespected.

□ □ □

Putin and I got home from our jaunt with Superman and mom told us she'd received a letter from Bob the social worker. Our food stamp application was on hold, pending further documentation. It was about mom's questionable marital status—was she really married to dad? She wasn't saying. I didn't expect her to.

Months before dad's bust and Frankie Jones's pregnancy, I came across a stray dog, a mutt with a bad paw limping on Capp Street. I brought it home, in love with its soft, defeated eyes. Mom wouldn't let me keep it—she borrowed a car and took the dog with her to Ocean Beach, over by Golden Gate Park. She pushed it out the door and drove away, shooting down the Great Highway until there was no dog, and no soft, defeated eyes in the rearview mirror. That was how we did things around here.

SEVEN

Once I got the news about Frankie Jones's deportation and the status of our food stamp application, I retired to the bathroom—the only place I could be alone and think clearly. I hunkered on the toilet seat and remembered what the old man had told me: "When you grow up, read Mayakovsky."

Mayakovsky was a Russian poet. He tore up his vocal cords reciting poetry to vast crowds. He'd snuffed himself with a gun. Moreover, he was a comrade in arms to the Bolsheviks—the old man's big brother had been a Bolshevik. A diehard revolutionary.

I was eight when the old man said to read Mayakovsky. I was already a seasoned gun thief. Cold-blooded, nimble-footed, and quick-witted. As time went on, I worked out the old man's advice wasn't only from him, but his Bolshevik brother too. A transmission from the motherland. In the spaces between Mayakovsky's words—the silences where the power of poetry thrived—in those spaces, I'd find freedom.

Frankie Jones and Mayakovsky would've loved each other. For she understood life's inner secrets. Some people went to prison. Some went to Bakersfield. If Mayakovsky wanted to kill himself, she'd pry the gun from his fingers, and murmur, sugar, it doesn't have to go down this way. In discussing poetry with Frankie, Mayakovsky would stress the new world was coming. Touched by Frankie's beauty and wisdom— she knew life's inner secrets—he would then compose the greatest poem ever written. In all creation. Solely for Frankie Jones.

□ □ □

The morning before the cops apprehended dad and me in Pacific Heights, Ronnie threw a brunch at his house and invited our family to it. He had a swimming pool in his backyard, a portable vinyl one. The kind that stank in the sun. Putin and I were stoked to go and use it.

Dad, mom, Putin, and I jetted to Ronnie's place on Blake Street in Berkeley. After securing dad's car with a padlock—he didn't want anyone liberating his guns from the back seat—we slinked into the patio where the brunch was going full blast. Ronnie presented us to his buddies, polyester-clad thieves like him and dad. I drooled over the picnic tables laden with platters of fried chicken, cold cuts, bowls of fruit, and pasta dishes. But there was no swimming pool. Ronnie had dismantled it, leaving a circle of dead grass. I felt like crying.

Bored with the adults—they were getting a head start on the day's drinking—the other kids at the brunch played with Putin and me. First off, I exhibited my missing front tooth. That got some laughs. We then dreamed up a game called pass-the-gun, a sport centered on the SKS rifle Ronnie had left in the yard. There was one rule: Everyone got an equal opportunity to dry-fire it.

When it was my turn to give the SKS to the next kid, a squabble erupted. I was reluctant to share the weapon—I wanted it for myself. It suited me. Its humble shape and size. A tiny-ass little white girl with yellow ribbons in her hair got upset. She bawled and wham: Ronnie scooped me up in his arms—dad was with him. They voted to incarcerate me in the garage.

"You're fucking up, kid. Chill out."

I was conducted into the unlit garage. Ronnie bolted the door shut from the outside. I whirled around. The fawn's eyes—eyes that reminded me of the dog's soft, defeated eyes—cornered me in the gloom. The animal poked its black nose between the baby crib's slats. Was I a threat to it?

"I'm not a threat to you," I giggled. "Only to myself."
The fawn snorted. It didn't like me.

Hours sailed by. I listened to the voices in my head.
Mom insisted I needed meds. The instructors at the
clinic said I should be in Napa State. The garage door
creaked open a tad before noon, letting in the sun's
brown rays. Ronnie and dad—drunk to the gills on
mimosas—teetered into the garage.

"Hey, there! We're letting you out!"

The deer's eyes widened. Dad bumbled to a crate of
AK-47 rifles and looked it over as I scurried past him
and Ronnie and the fawn out of the garage and into the
yard. Putin and the other kids were still playing pass-
the-gun with the SKS. I was reunited with them, no
hard feelings. And the light in the sky brightened until
our wee merry faces shined with beads of sweat.

Then dad and I went out and got arrested.

EIGHT

The last thing Superman said to us yesterday was that he and his boyfriend Tony—he was a janitor at the clinic—were hosting a shindig at their apartment in a few days. Putin and I were asked to come to it.

□ □ □

I was thinking about Mayakovsky in the morning as Putin and I hiked on Mission Street. Thinking how the poet would've been hard pressed to see anything good in the SWAT unit that was blanketing the sidewalk—a sea of blue uniforms ringed the homeless encampment beside the liquor store Superman had robbed. Putin glommed on to my shirtsleeve. "I've got something important to say to you."

I ceased breathing—I'd just heard payback. Ever since I nagged Putin for scaring the fawn, it had been coming my way. "What are you talking about?"

Putin's chipped off-white teeth glittered in the red smoky light. "Let me tell you. Everything you know about your past is a revisionist lie."

"For real?"

"Yes, it is."

"How do you know?"

"I'm a student of the past."

"You are?"

"That's correct. I know a lot."

My head was about to implode. "Let me guess. You know something about me."

"Maybe I do."

"And what is it?"

"Are you ready?"

"Ready for what?"

"Dad isn't your dad."

"You can't say that."

"I just did. You don't know who your dad is." Putin and I faced off nose to nose, his vinegary breath dampened my cheeks. "And mom doesn't know who it is either. That's why she hates you."

I squared my shoulders. "You're crazy. Prove it."

"I don't have to."

"That's it? What are your sources?"

"I refuse to disclose them. I'm no snitch."

"You won't verify your information?"

"Why should I? I'm not obliged to."

"That's dishonest. Really low."

"Tough titty."

"Did mom tell you? Was it her?"

"Dumb fuck." Putin emitted a high-pitched laugh. "Don't push your luck."

I let him have it. "You're an evil shit."

"Maybe I am. But I'm your mirror."

"The hell you are. Does mom hate you too?"

"You're so stupid. Where have you been?"

"She doesn't?"

"Of course not. She favors me. I'm her golden child."

"Oh, god." In that moment I saw the world for what it was. "Is this why you get more milk than I do?"

"Yes."

"And why you always get a birthday cake, even if I don't?"

"Yes. I pity you."

I was gobsmacked. All that history. All that psychological conflict. From a nine-year-old brat. My knees buckled, tears welled in my eyes. Dad wasn't my dad. I was not of his blood. Putin waited for me to blubber. I didn't, not then.

I kept a color snapshot of dad and mom next to my pillow. In the picture—taken in Marin under the shadow of Mount Tamalpais—dad cradled a modified Thompson submachine gun with a customized stock in his arms. His almost-white hair was plastered to his scalp; his red eyes were bright, happy with the Thompson. Mom posed by his side, her hairdo a shellacked platinum bob, her mouth black with lipstick.

I sat cross-legged at their feet.

Behind us a green balloon attached by a string to a folding chair had escaped its tether and had taken flight into the cloudless blue sky.

Balloon, balloon. I wanted to go with you.

Dad never educated Putin in gun stealing. Putin never accompanied him on a job. Now I knew why. Putin was the beloved son. The honeyed fruit of dad's seed. He got the extra glass of milk. The birthday cake. I was the ersatz son, from Christ knew where.

Let's be candid.

Burglary—dad had tutored me well. Every building I identified in the street, I cased it, to determine whether I could break into it. I measured rooftops with a scientist's eye. I cracked locks with a twist of my wrist. I ghosted unseen through barred doors. My fingers were as skilled as a concert pianist's fingers—just like Rachmaninov. Putin had no such talents, he was incapable of derring-do. But he was the golden child. Meant for loftier things than me.

Putin was destined for greatness.

Unlike myself.

Was I bitter? Perhaps.

NINE

Putin and I rolled up to Superman and Tony's soiree four nights later. Their front door was wide open, and we ushered ourselves inside. Our hosts sat on a pair of recycled car seats in the living room. Superman was in his pink track suit, Tony wore a matching blue one, to go along with his dyed black crew cut. They were busy kissing each other, and paid no attention to us.

Embarrassed by what Tony and Superman were doing, I focused on the cracks in their floor. Putin exploited the moment by snickering in my face. "You don't know who your real dad is. And mom is a short eyes."

"She's what?"

"You heard me, dumb ass."

"Don't say that."

"Make me."

"Keep talking smack, maybe I will."

"Try it, bozo. You ain't shit."

I wished he'd shut up. I went outside to the front stoop, the voices in my head very loud. I surveyed the lightless street—the dog with the soft, defeated eyes stared at me from the dark. With a canine's homing instinct, it had tracked me down. I whimpered, "Leave me alone, will you?"

Putin and the dog—I couldn't hack it.

I split from the party.

□ □ □

A car alarm was having a seizure on Mission Street—it wouldn't stop. I let myself into the old man's bungalow, and found him slumped in his rocking chair; a floor fan whirred in the living room's corner.

"Hey, old man. How you doing this evening?"

He blinked at me, the partisan who'd killed Nazis at the age of seventeen. The teenager that had jumped off a train full of Red Army soldiers dead from typhus, the only one left alive.

I had seen a picture of him taken in 1943. He was sixteen. In typical Russian fashion—because of the war—he looked fifty. I'd also mulled over a photograph of his Bolshevik brother. A handsome cat. Skin as smooth as ice cream. A mouth invented for love. Eyes that stopped for nothing on this earth.

I didn't resemble either of them.

The old man and his brother did not think alike. The brother swore by Karl Marx. The old man read Thomas Paine. One went to America, and labored in railroad yards. The other remained in the motherland—no one knew his fate.

The Bolshevik brother was in the constant hum of tension between the old man and the old lady about their relatives in Russia—everyone there had perished in the gulag, or from starvation and warfare with the Nazis.

The truth? The old lady ran the show at the bungalow because the old man couldn't see or hear too good. And she berated him. Dirty socks this, nail clippings that, cigarette butts in the bathroom sink. He never listened to her—he was too deep inside himself. The Bolsheviks. Nazis in the snow.

The old lady kvetched she'd had diarrhea—she had asked the old man to make her a cup of mint tea and a slice of toasted white bread. He gave her black tea so strong a pencil could stand up in it. That and a chunk of black bread topped with radishes.

I whispered to him: "Watch yourself, old man."

The first week the old man got to America he had a photo taken of himself in a cowboy costume at Coney Island. For the shot he was attired in fur-trimmed chaps. A bandanna looped around his neck. A lariat in his fist. A holstered six-gun riding on his hip. Cowboys reminded him of the Cossacks in Russia—he had a liking for Holly-wood Westerns. Once he and I watched *Tell Them Willie Boy Is Here*, a picture that starred Robert Blake and Robert Redford. Blake played Willie Boy, a Native American man who lived in Southern California a long time ago. The tale of how Willie Boy got in dutch with the cops and eluded them in the desert knocked me out of my socks. My friends and I resembled him. Not Redford—he was a lawman in the movie. But Willie Boy. We were on the run from everybody in the world. They'd get us eventually, but fuck it, we ran anyhow.

I bade farewell to the old lady and the old man. I mean-dered up Mission Street toward a homeless campsite that had attached itself to the SWAT checkpoint at Silver Avenue. Tarps and tents flush with the curb, dogs, and hard-eyed white men in broken shoes. A SWAT unarmored personnel carrier, aglow under the moth-clotted streetlights, swung out of the checkpoint, and nosed itself into the street. In one mouthful, dark-ness swallowed it.

□ □ □

I was back at the garage apartment when the landline rang near bedtime. I let the horn ring fifteen times. Mom screeched at me to answer it. I picked up the receiver.

It was Tony.

In a gruff voice he said Superman was sorry I'd left their wingding. He also said tens of thousands of pro-life Crusade for Jesus members—bused in from Arizona, Nevada, and Utah—had paraded up Market Street that afternoon. White folks and Mexicans chanting religious hymns and waving placards with pictures of fetuses. Tony added that Frankie Jones's mom and dad had been in the march.

While he talked, I thought about the old man in the cowboy costume at Coney Island. The way he'd smiled for his picture, glad to be in America. Tony said good night and hung up on me before I could tell him any of that.

TEN

"Did you find any treasures?"

The little white boy asked me that while he clutched his mother's hand, a large, young woman in a purple muumuu. It was the evening after Tony and Superman's bash. We were in the Safeway supermarket at Church and Market. I was there for the air conditioning—it was blazing outside. They had a shopping cart loaded with frozen pizzas. I took stock of the kid—he was half my height. I wanted to say it was a mean world—most of the good things had been taken. Some people went to prison. Some went to Bakersfield. There were no treasures. I blurted, "Yeah, I did. In aisle four. Keep your eyes peeled for them."

On top of everything else, the plainclothes cop the Lone Ranger had been warning everybody about—Lackner the undercover—was seen loitering near the Walgreens at Ninth and Market. A stocky gray cat in a sleeveless denim jacket, blue watch cap, and baggy jeans, his bearded face half-hidden behind imitation Gucci sunglasses. He was asking people about Superman and the liquor store robbery. I intended to steer clear of Lackner. I had enough problems—problems so weird, the air surrounding them bugged out in all directions—without him pestering me. The punk.

□ □ □

In the hush of night, houseflies made a racket and Borodin gushed from the living room radio as I was jarred into wakefulness by a nightmare—I'd been in a room crowded with unmasked people breathing all over me.

Hungover from the dream, I got out of bed and padded into the bathroom. I clicked on the light, and peered in the mirror. I appraised the hollows in my cheeks, the gaps between my teeth, and the eyes that never stopped scamming.

I saw fear in my own eyes. Black and luminous. The same fear I saw in dad's eyes. Ronnie's eyes. The Lone Ranger's eyes. Superman's too. Fear of the cops. Fear of getting snitched out. Fear of cracking up under the pressure. A fear that burned brightest when I was by myself. The badlands.

The ocean fog crept into the city on cat's paws almost every single day—tiptoeing inland from China Beach and spreading all the way to Telegraph Hill. Dad and I had emulated the fog in our work—we moved as quietly as it did through the houses we broke into.

Whenever I was inside a mini-mansion I made it a rule to lurk into a kid's room. Someone my age who had a dresser overflowing with fancy clothes. If dad was busy—in the den where the master of the house stored his guns—I'd sit on the kid's bed. I would eyeball his dresser—god knew I needed clothes. In my mind Frankenstein admonished me: Don't be naughty. Then Superman seethed in my ear: Do what you gotta do, fool. Take some clothes.

I never did.

I don't remember how many mini-mansions dad and I pillaged. At least two dozen. Dad was convinced break-ins were best executed by the light of day. A crime so obvious would never arouse suspicion—his strategy was why I was on probation, mandated by juvenile court to stay away from Pacific Heights for the next eight years, and he was bunking down in Muscupiabe tonight.

Dad's downfall had been inevitable. I initially got wind of it at Thanksgiving. He and I had broken into a Clay Street mini-mansion while the owners were at home—

dad had made a gross miscalculation, wrongly believing we'd be alone and unmolested to carry out our business. The owners were in the kitchen—we prowled on kitty-cat feet in the living room.

Dad pressed a finger to his lips. Shh.

I ignored his signal—to hell with dad, he could fend for himself. I carved a path to the front door. I unlocked it and lurched outside to the street. Then it was off to the races. Lyon. Baker. Broderick. Divisadero. Broadway. Pacific. Jackson. I sprinted downhill into the Western Addition—the streets disappeared under my feet quicker than a speeding bullet. But a voice in my head said over and over: Dad is a fucking lunatic. What's next?

□ □ □

Each one of mom's husbands had been a convict. Since dad—who wasn't my dad—was locked up again, she was writing letters to a prisoner at Pelican Bay. A cat affiliated with the BGF—the Black Guerrilla Family. Someone who was twenty years younger than her. As icing on the cake, dad had accidentally left behind a pistol in our apartment—I had taken possession of it.

When I was seven—three months into my apprenticeship in gun thievery—dad and Ronnie liberated a container of gelignite from a military base in the Central Valley. They drove to a ravine north of Napa State to experiment with the explosive, to consider its potential, what it could do. Dad lost three fingers on his left hand.

Dad adapted to the loss of his digits by relearning how to shoot. Instead of using his disabled hand, he taught himself to steady a rifle in the crook of his elbow. Plus, dad acquired a troublesome habit—he loved to rub his polished finger stumps on my head, a gesture that, in all honesty, I never cottoned to.

Putin was emotionally scarred by dad's accident. My brother changed overnight from a lamb into a wolf. And now the golden child was building a bomb. He'd told me it was coming along just fine—he was in the process of choosing the proper materials for it. "I'm doing it right," said Putin.

I flicked off the bathroom light, and slunk to the bedroom.

ELEVEN

I slid into my cot with dad's pistol, allowing its well-oiled steel weight to rest on my chest. I tossed and turned in between the sheets, unable to conk out. I wondered how Frankie Jones was doing in Bakersfield. That reminded me of what the Lone Ranger told Putin at the clinic:

"I was in El Pocho last spring, the place on South Van Ness, and this Crusade boy was there bragging about his money. Then Frankie Jones came up to him. Her fingers did a tango in his pocket, relieving the clod of everything he had—he never knew what hit him! Just talked his madness while Frankie went outside and gave the paper to a wino. She said it was a little gift from Jesus."

I looked over at Putin. He snored face down on his cot, the sheets covering his head to ward off the mosquitos. For the life of me, I didn't know what mom was doing in our room the other night. Putin was not a credible witness—no one listened to a kid.

Mom would never let me know who my father was—it wasn't her style. But she had said dad who was not my dad swung both ways. In plain English, he was bisexual. She maintained it started during his first stint at Muscupiabe—he was punked in the pen. "The poor, poor man," she'd gloated.

Dad's car always had rifles in the trunk, and on the back seat and floor. Countless times I was with him as the cops pulled alongside us at a stoplight. Dad looking straight ahead. The cops looking at him. Stolen guns everywhere. The light would turn to green, and the cops would rumble up the street. Dad would then pat me on the knee, and purr: "Now, now. That wasn't so bad, was it?"

The queer thing was dad never garnered a profit from stealing guns. We'd snagged a million pistols and rifles in our forays. But dad didn't earn squat.

It was Ronnie's doing—he'd rooked us.

Last summer Ronnie hipped dad to an unoccupied mini-mansion in St. Francis Wood—the owners were on vacation in Europe—and the house teemed with antique guns worth big bucks. That's what Ronnie said.

Neither dad nor I had done any business in St. Francis Wood—it was on the south side of the city, miles from our traditional hunting grounds. St. Francis Wood was virgin turf for us. Dad was keen to go there. I wasn't.

Seventy-two hours later dad and I were in front of our target zone. A pastel pink two-story Tudor parked under a massive redwood tree. Dad took a peek at the place, and grumbled, "Yeah, no, yeah, let's do this job. Here we go now." Silently, we treaded across a gravel driveway. Dad gave me a boost onto a trellis overgrown with purple and white bougainvillea—I was lighter than a feather. I scampered up the metal latticework to the second story. I unlatched a window and leaped into a dusty and silent room. I immediately knew something was hinky.

Ronnie had given us a bum steer—as usual.

This house had no guns.

The place smelled of parchment paper and oil paintings.

Not cordite and gun oil.

Then dad shouted from outside the police were coming down the street. I scrabbled out the window, and while I gripped the trellis—sweating the cops would nick me—I mashed my face into the sweet-smelling bougainvillea and imagined everything was a dream I'd never wake up from.

A year ago dad nailed a raccoon in the Presidio with his trusty .22 Ruger. He skinned the animal and home-tanned the hide in our living room. As a token of affection—rare for him—he gifted me with the trophy. I stashed the hide under my mattress until it attracted ants. So I put it outside on the stoop, but the neighbor's cat ran off with it.

Did dad love me? No one knew his mind. Least of all himself. He had a nineteenth-century-European view of children—I was a source of free labor. I had to be good for something. And I was. I was a gun thief par excellence.

I'd wanted to please dad.

But he held me responsible for the Pacific Heights bust.

I had failed him.

Dad had failed me too. For Christmas he'd promised me a gun rack. It was a big deal. A gun rack of your own was a status symbol—it separated you from the amateurs and poseurs.

To dad's chagrin, Putin abhorred guns. The golden child loathed the world of Thompson submachine guns. However, I, the ersatz son, had been comfortable in that world. Unfortunately, dad boomeranged to the joint.

I never got a gun rack.

□ □ □

I'd run across another photograph of the old man's Bolshevik brother. In the pic he wore an army tunic and a forage cap festooned with a red star. He gazed past the camera, chin tilted and mouth pursed, his eyes riveted on the new world.

Once upon a time the old man showed me a letter his brother sent him from Russia. The years had yellowed the paper it was written on. The inked scrawl was in Cyrillic: "There you are in America, eating crumbs from the capitalist table."

He was right. No food stamps yet.

I curled my finger around the pistol's trigger.

The dog with the soft, defeated eyes barked and barked itself hoarse outside the bedroom window.

I floated off to sleep.

TWELVE

One evening after the party in Glen Canyon, Frankie
Jones had dinner with her boyfriend at his family's
Pacific Heights mansion. His parents sat her down in
their living room with the fluffy white merino wool
rug and the Picasso print on the wall and asked what
was going on. The dad hunched over in a plush leather
chair and targeted her with his flat eyes. Frankie made
the mistake of telling him and his wife the truth—she
thought she was pregnant.

Nobody said anything.

Dinner was served by the maid. The first course, oysters
with lemon sauce. Then came walnut-stuffed organic
chicken and roasted potatoes. Her boyfriend scarfed a
plateful with his head lowered, his father and mother
at the other end of the table. Frankie had no appetite,
and excused herself to use the bathroom. She wandered
into the hallway, followed that for a bit, before she did
a detour to the master bedroom.

To see what was in there.

She wasn't disappointed. A wall-length window

commanded a view of the Golden Gate Bridge and the San Francisco Bay. A double king-sized bed boasted red satin sheets. Best was the walk-in closet—larger than a hospital ward. Without a second thought, she plunged into it, losing herself in rows of Italian designer clothes. Brioni. Loro Piana. Zegna.

Frankie was cocooned in silk dresses and cashmere suits—she breathed in the perfumed fabrics—protected by cashmere and silk from the outside world. Nobody knew where she was. No one could put their mitts on her tits. Or cup her ass. She felt the baby inside her. You don't know what you're doing, she told herself, don't worry. The baby will let you know—it's your compass.

She then detected footsteps—it had to be the maid. Frankie backpedaled out of the closet and the master bedroom. She oozed into the hall, inched over the carpet to the bathroom, but plowed head-on into her boyfriend's dad before she reached it. He latched his eyes on her, like he'd caught her doing something wrong. Admittedly, she had rifled through a jewelry box sitting on his wife's bureau. She'd pocketed an emerald-studded brooch, three diamond bracelets, and a pair of ruby earrings. But she had doubts about the theft. So she put the jewels back. Maybe the next time. He deciphered that in her eyes. How she thought about things. How unhidden she was, everything on the surface, for everyone to know. And he shouted at her to get the fuck out of his home. She didn't, he'd call the cops on her.

The maid hustled Frankie from the house to the street gate. The glinting chandelier lighting in the mansion's dormer windows mocked the pregnant girl. Ha ha. You're never coming to this place again.

Frankie adjusted her mask, and trekked southward on Divisadero. She was at Sacramento Street when a coyote with silver-gray fur and amber-yellow eyes streaked across the sidewalk, and weaved in and out of the shadows. Frankie whistled, "I'm a coyote too! Just like you!" The animal froze in mid-stride, glanced over its bony shoulder, held her in a long yellow stare, then it loped into the dark.

THIRTEEN

How could I explain the badlands to Putin? I couldn't. He'd have to find out for himself what they were about. Him and the bomb he was assembling.

□ □ □

High noon on Wednesday. It was turning out to be another lame day with nothing to eat when two SWAT policemen confronted Putin and me next to the Roxie on Sixteenth Street. They wanted to know what we were up to. I said we were en route to the clinic for our Jesus sessions. A lie because we were playing hooky. Then I was accused—not Putin—of shoplifting at the Whole Foods store in the Haight-Ashbury. I was yanked off my feet, and cuffed.

I was handled with kid gloves, and transported downtown in a squad car to the jail at 850 Bryant. It was rush hour—lots of incoming arrestees. Getting booked lasted an eternity. My clothing was impounded. I spread my butt cheeks for a squirt of DDT powder. I was tossed into the holding cell, a gray concrete box that bubbled over with dudes. A white guy stripped down to his boxers explained his situation to me. "I'm not cutting my hair again. I do that, it won't grow back. I'm going bald."

Somebody in the booking room discovered they had a juvenile in the holding cell, namely me. It was a bad flub—I was supposed to have been single-celled, so I wouldn't get raped. Anyone in administration uncovered the fuck-up, heads would get lopped off.

Rather than transferring me to juvie, since I hadn't been charged with anything—the shoplifting bit was a sham—the cops kicked me loose in the dead of night. But to punish me, they didn't give back my clothes. I got somebody else's belongings from the jail's property room. Smelly flip-flops, and a pair of red spandex bicycle shorts meant for a six-year-old girl.

I headed homeward, toddling along Folsom Street, the spandex shorts riding up my ass crack as the sky got light. The sun crested the rooftops, accompanied by a string of ravens beginning the perilous journey over the crosstown freeway to Pacific Heights—for pickings were much better up there than south of Market.

I turned into our driveway—five unmasked SWAT cops armed with beanbag guns stormed into the next-door apartment. They came back out with a Black woman—our neighbor—shouting at the top of her lungs. "Get your fucking hands off me!" The cops forced her to the curb—she fought them every step of the way. Another cop jammed a spit hood over her head to strangle her cries.

An ambulance came—four masked white medics bailed out and spread-eagled the woman on the pavement. They pinned her arms and legs to the ground, then injected her in the thigh with a drug that made her froth at the mouth. She convulsed and bucked her head. Her eyes spun in their sockets like she'd just spoken to god.

But he didn't hear her.

The cops and the medics strapped the woman—wearing the spit hood—onto a gurney. She was crammed into the ambulance, and away it went through the smoke to Napa State. I trembled, older than I'd ever been.

FOURTEEN

Hours later, I still trembled. Yesterday was dad's—who was not my dad—fifty-second birthday. There were no presents, and no celebration. Not at Muscupiabe.

Indifferent to the fact that the cops had detained me in 850 Bryant, mom utilized dad's birthday to wax about him. "Your father is a good-humored man. Slow to anger. Eager to please. Willing to play second-best to Ronnie. And look at what it got him. He's written me a letter from Muscupiabe. He says I'm guilty of having sex, not only with other men, but with dogs too. Sex with dogs. This is what he says. And he wants us to visit him. Maybe someday. Maybe not."

Mom was correct. Dad and Ronnie were quite the couple. Ronnie was a foot shorter than dad and twice as broad. He affected antique polyester leisure suits, flared pants, wide shirt lapels. High-grade polyester, not the cheap kind. Ronnie had badgered dad, like his tacky clothes gave him the license to boss dad. I'd heard through the grapevine from the Lone Ranger, who always had his ear to the ground, Ronnie was worried dad would snitch him out. I didn't care a whit for Ronnie, not since he'd locked me in his garage with the fawn—the damn animal had given me fleas.

□ □ □

I was in bed that night thinking about birthday cakes, big ones slathered with coconut puree. The bedroom door swung open—mom blitzed into the room. She flipped on the overhead light, twirled around, and positioned herself between Putin's cot and my cot. "Your grandfather is gone. He left a note saying he's going south to the desert. I'm sorry I didn't tell you sooner. I thought it was best not to."

Putin turned his face to the wall.

I sniveled from under the sheets: "Go away!"

Don't make me say it again—I was scared.

Mom's voice was strictly Napa State.

It seemed—mom said—the old lady had been harassing the old man, giving him grief about his manners, the way he attacked the food on his plate at supper. He ate with his hands, and made sucking noises because of his ill-fitting dentures.

Fine. He wasn't polite—too bad.

The old man was born in Kiev. A city in flames when he

was a youth. A city that was on fire today. It was no secret to me why he went to the desert—he was trying to kill himself. The hard way. The long way. The Russian way.

I pictured his Salem cigarettes. His dog-eared copy of James Fenimore Cooper's *The Last of the Mohicans*. His borscht with a dollop of sour cream.

What hell.

The desert was a sweep of agave plants, Gila monsters, and arroyos dotted with the unmarked graves of refugees who'd attempted the jornada to El Norte—the border patrol would never find the wily partisan out there.

The next night, still freaked out by the old man's disappearance, I trooped over to Superman and Tony's place to find out what they were doing. I discovered them standing at arm's length from each other in the living room. Tony keened, "I tested positive."

Superman wagged his head in disgust, ambled to his record collection, selected a well-worn Marvin Gaye album, and put it on the turntable—the speakers blasted the intro to "What's Going On." Superman then extended a hand to Tony. Grudgingly, Tony eased into his arms. Together, hugging each other, they bumped into the room's damp, hot walls.

Superman was moody, what with Tony being positive. He squinted over his boyfriend's shoulder to where I sat, having made myself comfy in one of their raggedy-ass car seats. Superman shot me the evil eye. "What are you doing here? It's late. You got a problem? You got OCD? And you talk weird. All those big words. You a snake in the grass? Superman believes you are."

Superman disentangled himself from Tony's arms, and hightailed it out of the living room into the kitchen. He futzed under the sink until he came up with a short-handled axe. He hefted the axe, admired its blade, then burst into the living room.

He flew right at me.

I catapulted from the car seat, skipped by Superman's reach, then dove out the ground floor living room window, shattering it before landing ass backward on the sidewalk. I scrambled to my feet, and hobbled toward Mission Street—the dog with the soft, defeated eyes still pursued me, nipping at my pants.

FIFTEEN

I darted to the garage apartment—mom and Putin weren't there. I charged into the bedroom, reached under my cot, and recited a magic spell. Abracadabra. Open sesame. Shazam. Voilà. I stood upright, dad's pistol in my clammy hand.

I was going to the rodeo.

I rocketed from the apartment and tramped down Capp Street, overtaking the Victoria Theatre—the rats nesting in the curbside palm trees marked my progress. Bits of fog crowned the Sixteenth Street BART station as street people hawked bus transfers. "Late night! Late night!"

Minutes later, I was at Tony and Superman's dump. The two of them sat on the living room floor. The axe was under a car seat. Nobody had swept up the broken glass from the window. Superman wasn't unhappy with my presence, maybe even a bit glad. "Well, well, guess who's here? Superman ain't retracting what he said. You're a snake in the grass."

Tony begged me with his reddened eyes to ignore Superman.

What would Mayakovsky do in my shoes?
He'd terminate Superman. No questions asked.
No quarter given.
But I wasn't a poet. I hadn't even had sex yet.
Deflated by that realization, I exited the living room.

I stalked out of their pad, and glanced at the fire-black, moonless sky splashing over me—the evening marked the end of one thing, and the beginning of something else.

◻ ◻ ◻

A month into my twelfth year, dad completed his first sentence at Muscupiabe. While he was gone, I had reverted to a primitive, younger version of myself. Secretive, prone to temper tantrums. Anorexic. Given to bruxism.

Out of the pen, dad resumed burgling guns. He bullied me into rejoining him. This time, he reassured me, there would be no mistakes. He crowed the jobs we'd pull would make us proud of ourselves. Expert craftsmen. The crème de la crème of our vocation. Now that I was nearing thirteen—with the sagacity of my age—I knew he'd duped me. Wasn't it always this way? When you were a youngster? You thought you'd conquered the world. But you knew diddly-squat.

Though dad was a mediocre outlaw—top-flight villains didn't do time at Muscupiabe—he wasn't one of the smash-and-grab criminals the mayor decried at her press conferences about law and order in the city. He didn't rampage through Union Square jewelry stores—dad had nothing in common with those guys. He may not have been the craftsman he said he was—what a joke—but dad was a performance artist with an unwitting eye for poetry.

□ □ □

Ronnie, dad, and I used to test-fire stolen weapons at Point Reyes in western Marin, down a gorge a mile east of the ocean. Legend had it Native Americans camped there in the nineteenth century. I felt their spirits whenever I was in the gorge with Ronnie and dad. In the rocks and trees and earth. In the earth that was taking dad and Ronnie. That would take me. I did not want this—I didn't want to end up like dad.

The year dad was sprung from the pen he initiated me into the mysteries of automatic weapons—target practice with his modified Thompson in the hills west of Napa State. I received gunpowder burns from mis-handling the machine gun. The spent cartridges seared my fingers. Dad affectionately whacked me upside my head, and brayed, "It's good for you, sonny. It'll make you strong. Just like me."

I had gunpowder residue on my arms the evening mom escorted me to a cinema house in the Richmond District to view an adult movie, inappropriate for a kid. A revival of *Scorpio Rising* by Kenneth Anger. The film was dreamlike, a strange planet. Breathless, I panted in the near-deserted theater, "Yes, oh, god, yes, this is where I live!"

PART TWO

IN THE NEW WORLD

SIXTEEN

I was only as good as the people around me.

Superman rang up on the landline the next morning to mellow out things between us—he professed he hadn't intended to kill me with his axe. "Superman was just having a bad time. He was tripping. It ain't no thing." I repaid his candor by confessing my pistol had been unloaded—dad never left any bullets.

Superman went on to say sometime in the last few days Frankie Jones's parents had left the city. Tony sussed their place was deserted, and went to give a closer look. He came across a note tacked to the door: "Moved to Oklahoma."

Subsequent to my chat with Superman, I skulked into the kitchenette. I had a look-see out the window—the neighbor's avocado tree cast a shadow on our driveway, a shadow that didn't move in the brown sunlight, a shadow that played dead on the ground. I kept tabs on it until an unmarked white county sedan showed up. I was spooked it was the cops—Bob the social worker emerged from the car in his camouflage safari suit.

Mom nudged open the screen door to greet Bob. She was wrapped in a tatty pink chenille bathrobe, her hair peroxided into an orange-white fireball. "Good morning," she tittered. "I'd offer you something to eat or drink, but we have nothing. So there." She laughed, bittersweet and low—channeling Julie Christie as Lara in *Doctor Zhivago*.

The social worker's eyes bore into the little woman in the scruffy bathrobe. Spurred on by his attention, she pirouetted in the living room, the linoleum floor carpeted with secondhand paperbacks, the books she read to soothe her because the antidepressants didn't always work. Novels by Turgenev, Gogol, and Gorky she'd purchased for a quarter apiece at a Noe Valley garage sale.

Bob glanced at the books, and sniggered.

He was my mortal enemy.

Any man who sniggered at Gogol was someone to fear.

Bob told mom she had an excellent chance to get her food stamp application approved. She merely had to report to the welfare office and sign additional papers.

He made it sound like we had won the lottery. That we shouldn't ask for more than that. Not from him, not from anyone, not from god, not from life itself.

Putin blundered into the living room, and stuttered in impenetrable English, "I'm creating a bomb. The biggest and the best. It's magnificent. The most wondrous thing on earth."

My heart fluttered and soared with joy. Putin hadn't opened his mouth since the old man went to the desert.

Bob didn't understand a word my brother said. "What the hell is he talking about?"

"It's a poem," I assured him. "A beautiful poem."

Voices went round and round in my head. Frankie Jones said to Mayakovsky that Pacific Heights was a place without linoleum or stucco where no one ever died. He responded by avowing paradise was everywhere.

The declarations of the pickpocket and the poet mingled in my brain while Putin entertained Bob with incomprehensible gibberish about his bomb. The social worker ogled mom—he was desperate to dip his wick in her. I closed my eyes. The new world was coming. Any moment now.

SEVENTEEN

Putin said he cut through Dolores Park earlier today on his way to the clinic. He'd crossed paths with Lackner the undercover. The plainclothes cop had been hanging out by the park's tennis courts. Lackner had rousted Putin—what do you know about the liquor store caper? Who is Superman?

Putin quizzed me: Why did we live like this?

I told him the truth. I didn't know. I really didn't.

The instructors at the clinic challenged us every day: Do you believe in Jesus? Yes or no. Nonbelievers— heathens—were singled out, and punished by lockdowns in the prayer room. The Lone Ranger had been sent there eight times in the previous two weeks.

The instructors preached Jesus's loving hand touched everything in the world. The Marin County fire that raged from San Rafael to Fairfax. The people overdosing on fentanyl in the city. Everyone with the virus. Everybody at Napa State.

Frankenstein hyped the line Jesus considered every child in his kingdom as sacred. I didn't buy it. Frankenstein wasn't talking about me, Putin, the Lone Ranger, or Superman. In her book, we were the devil's urchins.

I'd undergone a battery of psychological tests at the clinic. The results? I had a disease. The term for it was conduct disorder. The instinctive urge to disrupt and violate social norms. The instructors were horrified by the diagnosis. My Jesus sessions were tripled in number. Many a day was spent on my knees in the prayer room alongside the Lone Ranger.

Crusade for Jesus security guards had pummeled a kid in the clinic's cafeteria because he'd worn a Mexican flag over his shoulders. They belted him senseless with their collapsible batons. A scuffle broke out—some kids threw food at the guards who, in retaliation, pepper sprayed them.

Putin and I elected to skip the afternoon's Jesus sessions—things were too hairy at the clinic. He and I got together with Superman at Mission and Duboce, then we hoofed it past the boarded up Walgreens and down Mission Street while the voices in my head screamed bloody murder.

Superman let us know, due to a mix-up with the mail—he lived two doors down from Frankie's old place—he'd received a postcard addressed to her from her cousins in Oklahoma. They'd written it was terrific Frankie was having a baby with a Crusade for Jesus member. A religious boy. He'd be a good father. Had the wedding been scheduled yet? Were they invited?

Putin confirmed mom got a phone call from Muscupiabe, from our dad who was not my dad. According to Putin, dad was getting transferred to a maximum security pen further north. Someplace near the border with Oregon. Dad had asked us to visit him before that went down. Putin said to me, "What do you think?"

I didn't answer him. Not with words, in any case.

I bayed—the voices in my head were too loud.

Stop it. Stop it. Stop it.

□ □ □

At sundown my brother and I doubled back to the garage apartment—Superman had ditched us because I wouldn't quit screaming. I encountered a letter from welfare on the kitchenette counter. It was about our benefits. Welfare gave mom enough money for Putin and me to get a new pair of pants once a year, the cheapest jeans at Target.

Last winter. The memory of washing my welfare jeans

in the kitchenette sink was punctuated by the recollection of scrubbing my underwear. Lonely piss-stained briefs. I put them on a coat hanger to dry next to the living room wall heater where they steamed up the windows. But heeding the rhyme and delirium of the seasons, spring chasing winter, I ceased wearing underwear altogether—never to wash them again under mom's disapproving glare.

No underwear created a problem each time I got taken into custody. Whether it was juvie or county jail, the cops didn't like it. They confiscated your clothes during booking and saw you had nada to cover up your private parts. The other prisoners didn't give a hoot—they had their own worries.

Putin yammered at me, "Mom's not here, what are we gonna do for supper?" I gibbered, "Do we have any eggs?" "There's a bag of powdered ones," he rejoined. I whooped, "Hallelujah! I'll cook you an omelet with toast." "There's no bread," he griped. "Nice," I retorted. "No toast. So what's new."
    I did the eggs.
    They tasted like glue.
    We ate in silence.
    Putin washed the dishes. I dried them.
    Nighttime came on strong. Stars were invisible, the

moon painted in yellow smoke. I hung the dish towel on its hook and peeped out the kitchenette window. I looked at the pedestrians in the street. Their faces blurred under the streetlights. I was a stranger to them—the people who loved me hadn't been born yet. I was at the window, waiting for them.

I hoped I wouldn't have to wait too long.

EIGHTEEN

I was toying with my ankle bracelet in the bathroom the following morning. Putin sneaked up from behind, jabbed me in the ribs and stammered, "I finally got it right. It's a monumental achievement. Nobody has ever done what I did. Nobody ever will. Come and I'll show you."

A jag of anxiety knifed me—Putin's breath was terrible.

Putin guided us to our room. He got on his knees, rummaged under his cot, and dredged up a pair of mom's coarse black woolen babushka stockings—they were stuffed with rectangular blocks of styrofoam. Putin straightened up, belted the lumpy thing about his waist, and tied the ends into a knot. His pink face beamed with pride. "Here it is. This is it. I put a lot of time and work into it. But I did it good. I used the best ingredients. This is my bomb."

I grinned at my brother—what a genius.

Putin was excited about his bomb—he'd convinced himself it was a masterpiece—so we dashed around the corner to show it to Tony and Superman. The sidewalk reeked of fried food and rotting trash. Mosquitos were everywhere. I sneezed, then readjusted my new mask, which was someone else's mask I'd found in a free box by our driveway.

Superman hailed us from his stoop. "If it ain't the wild boys!" He was enthroned in a car seat, his bare feet propped on an overturned milk crate. Putin paused by the stoop and cautioned him. "Don't you start nothing with me, Superman. I'm dangerous. This here," he gestured at the styrofoam-packed black babushka stockings girded around his hips, "this is a bomb. None better. It's devised from the finest components known to humankind."

Superman adored it—a tic in his right eye went bananas. He clapped his hands. "You got a bomb? A little peewee like you? Bravo! That's slick, my man!"

Putin blushed, delighted with Superman's praise.

◻ ◻ ◻

One sweltering day in June—a week before we got busted in Pacific Heights—dad and I were in his car on an unpaved road beyond Napa State. The back seat was cluttered with double-barreled shot-guns and bolt-action hunting rifles. The Thompson submachine gun in the front seat between us. Dad's mutilated hand was draped over the steering wheel, the other rested on my shoulder. "Listen, kid. You and me better talk about who your father is and who I am. There are problems. Lots of them."

But then dad spied a bobcat in the roadside bushes. Without slowing down, he reached for a vintage M-1 carbine. He pushed the carbine's barrel out the driver's window, and while he steered the car with his knees, sprayed five quick rounds at the bewildered animal.

Our conversation was forgotten.

The tang of gunpowder up my nose.

I'm pretty sure he wanted to tell me he wasn't my father that day. And I'm certain I didn't give him the high sign the cops were coming when they collared us in Pacific Heights because he didn't. Honestly? I believed Putin's bomb was a step in the right direction.

◻ ◻ ◻

On the heels of our discussion with Superman, Putin and I trundled toward the plaza at Sixteenth and Mission. Putin grandiosely predicted his bomb would change the world. "I'll make shit fly," he trumpeted. "People are always trying to put me down. They think I'm a loser. But I'll get respect now. You wait and see."

NINETEEN

Frankie Jones dialed the baby's daddy's house from her aunt and uncle's place in Bakersfield. The maid took the call—she recognized Frankie's voice. Frankie asked if the boyfriend was at home. The maid dithered, "No, he doesn't live here. He's at school in New York." Frankie sensed the wall in front of the maid's words— no, he doesn't live here—and she high-jumped the wall. She inquired, "Do you have a number for him?" Before she got a response, the phone changed hands. The baby's daddy's father came on the line. He wailed if Frankie didn't leave his son alone, he'd get a court order to make sure she did.

Frankie then phoned Tony. He answered on the third ring and railed at her, "You're ruining your life, girl-friend. That Crusade boy did you dirt. What he did, Crusade boys do to all kinds of girls. So what did you expect? That he'd want the kid? Why are you keeping that damn baby? Your dad fucked with you, not letting you get a procedure."

Frankie snorted, "You should talk. What the hell

are you doing with Superman? I've been around that maniac all my life. He talks about himself like he's someone else. Is that what you want? To come home one day to find he's dead on the floor and somebody stole the furniture?"

Tony cut in. "Okay, okay. I've got a plan. A good one. I'll borrow Superman's whip and we'll go where someone can do something about the baby. That's it! We'll go to Los Angeles. You can get it taken care of there."

Frankie was stern. "I should've done that while I had the chance. But I can't do it now. I'm too far along. And don't change the subject. You know the only reason Superman didn't get done for the liquor store thing was because the surveillance cameras over there crapped out."

Her friend sighed. "I give up. You're too hardheaded. You go ahead and have that baby. I can't stop you."

The final time Frankie called the baby's daddy's house, the maid answered again. She gave the horn to the mother. A high-strung woman who was always polite and well-dressed. She let Frankie know in a wavery voice, since she persisted in trying to contact her son, a temporary restraining order had been issued to curb her. Frankie caressed her stomach and said she and her damn husband could do whatever they wanted, but it didn't change a thing. An unexpected child was coming—life would be different for it.

TWENTY

Putin had unveiled his bomb—our lives turned upside down. Mom scrounged together enough pennies to buy a gallon of milk at the liquor store. She came back to the apartment with it and instructed Putin and me to limit ourselves to a glass of milk per day. Better yet, to make it last, maybe every other day.

□ □ □

In the deepest part of the night there was a mouse-like clatter in the kitchenette. Tiny noises which spelled big trouble. I roused myself and went to investigate what they were about. I barged into mom at the fridge. She was glugging milk from the carton, getting it on her robe. Her eyes howled: Stay the fuck away from me.

Seeing mom all meshugga in the kitchenette agitated me. I pulled on my pants and escaped out the front door. Swatting mosquitos, I traipsed south on Shotwell. The cops were tear-gassing a homeless bivouac that had spilled into the street. I got a whiff of the gas and coughed and coughed until I gagged.

I circled home at daybreak. Mom was half-awake on the living room couch, her ratty chenille bathrobe spread over her marbled thighs. She announced, "I'm not pretty."

Heavy-lidded, she simpered at me. A brown-toothed smile that intimated, should I tell her it wasn't so, she'd believe it. Things would be good between us, bad things forgotten. I didn't take the bait.

"What? You no think I'm pretty?"

I sat on the floor by the living room window, the rising sun for company. My heart thudded harder than a drum machine, for mom was not friendly.

"You no listen. I'm not pretty?"

She crossed her legs—the bathrobe parted, and exposed her fabled bush. I forced myself to stare out the window.

Noon hour. I was in the Safeway supermarket on Market Street. Like a phantom—how plainclothes cops always did it—Lackner the undercover put in an appearance in the produce section. I tried to frame the scenario like I was outside of it. I reconnoitered the cop from somewhere far off and safe. But as it happened, he stood a few feet away from me.

Who robbed the liquor store? Where is Superman?

I moved over to the grapes bin. Lackner fondled a papaya and acted nonchalant. Fuck him. I wasn't going to talk about the robbery. I didn't give a damn how much money was stolen—the Lone Ranger said he'd heard from confidential sources, which meant Superman himself, it was fifty racks.

I waltzed toward the oranges.

Nope. I wasn't talking. Not in this lifetime.

□ □ □

The living room radio tinkled a Rimsky-Korsakov opera at sunset. The atmosphere ripe to present my case. I approached mom in the kitchenette—she was at the stove, frying potatoes with paprika. I was blunt with her, no varnish.

"I want a birthday cake this year. It's time I got one."

She lifted one eyelid higher than the other—a holdover from an old bout with Bell's palsy—and clenched her jaw, a sure-fire sign she was about to cuss me out. You? A little shit? A birthday cake? But she calmly said, "Maybe. It depends. Money, no?"

She promised little—I embraced it.

I went for a stroll to celebrate my victory. I passed General Hospital on Potrero Avenue as Department of Corrections guards unloaded a van of infected prisoners in the parking lot. The guards corralled the gowned and masked convicts, waist chains clanking, into the emergency room. Maybe dad who was not my dad was among them. Among the pale, sick men fading into the hospital. He wasn't—Muscupiabe was hundreds of miles away. I was sad. It would've been great to talk to him. God, how dumb I was—he wasn't even my father.

◻ ◻ ◻

Furniture movers came by our neighbor's apartment while I was out and they carted off her possessions. Putin had asked them what was up—they didn't tell him much, only that she was in lockdown at Napa State. And she'd be there for a long, long time. Putin's analysis was precise: "She's in the gulag, man."

TWENTY-ONE

Life went much faster when Putin started to wear his bomb. There was something about the bomb I couldn't quite put my finger on. Something that got under my skin. Something that creeped me out. Early one morning, he and I humped it down windswept San Carlos Street and stumbled into a SWAT foot patrol. The cops wanted to know what Putin had around his waist. Mom's babushka stockings brimming with styrofoam. By the grins on their faces they didn't get what it was. The cops laughed. It was a big joke to them. A retarded kid with his crappy toy. But I was anxious— Putin's bomb had begun to scare the hell outta me.

□ □ □

Noontime that day found me and Putin with Superman while he gassed up his whip—a primer-gray '67 Malibu with twenty-two inch rims—at a station on Guerrero at the corner of Sixteenth. An apple red Tesla with black competition stripes drew up next to us—five athletic Crusade boys surfaced from the car. They were blond and sunburned in surfer shorts and silk T-shirts, their necks and wrists adorned with gold chains that attracted all the sunlight. Their cherubic faces not yet overtaken by the ruptured blood vessels of cocaine and Xanax abuse, the habits of their parents.

They strutted by the gas pumps.

I was pissed. Those chumps knew the dickhead that fucked over Frankie Jones. Furthermore, they waggled their fingers at Putin and jeered he was a Russian faggot with his toy bomb. A little punk. A pussy. Their jive ended when Superman shoved one of them to the cement. He reached down, grabbed the kid's gold chain, ripped it from his neck, and lobbed the gold into a trash can.

The other Crusade boys mobbed us.

Hooting they were gonna cream our asses.

A solitary glance from Superman—promising a descent into quicksand—paralyzed them. Shoeless, he demonstrated fake, poorly executed karate footwork for their benefit.

"C'mon, baby! Superman wants to have fun! Let's do it!"

His invitation—spiced with a peal of manic giggling—sealed the bargain. The Crusade boys beat a swift retreat to the Tesla. They clambered into their ride, and burned rubber out of the station up Sixteenth Street. The sun leered at them from the smoke as a voice warbled in my head: Frankie Jones, Frankie Jones. Superman sends you his love.

TWENTY-TWO

Anything in front of us was better than what we'd left behind. Another smoky day puttered by. Though I didn't want to get too chummy with him, not since he came at me with the axe, Superman asked me over to his crib, and I said yes. He told me to come by myself.

The second I got to his place, Superman gabbled about a .32 revolver, a Saturday night special that'd been employed to rob convenience stores in North Beach, four in the last month. "Superman needs to sell this thing for a friend. You know the Lone Ranger? So, you want the piece? Superman will give it to you for seventy-five bucks. It's a bargain."

Coming out of the closet had been difficult for Superman. For a start, his reputation as a tough guy had been at stake. Meeting Tony dispelled his qualms. No one was more butch than Tony—anyone that queer-baited him risked a beatdown. Tony had given Superman the courage and love he needed to accept himself for who he was. I said, "No thanks, Superman. I don't want the gun. I'm cool."

Superman's dull green eyes sliced into me. "You ain't cool, young blood. Take it from someone who knows what cool is. That's Superman."

Miffed by my rejection, Superman reverted to talking about himself in first person—he hadn't done it in months. He showered me with further insults. "Peewee, I predict you'll kill yourself. I see that in my crystal ball. I'm very serious about this. You've got the complexion for it. Sallow. Like you're righteously constipated."

That was swell.

I had the complexion for suicide.

Because I was constipated.

Speaking of guns, the last anyone heard of Ronnie, the fawn had escaped his garage and had taken refuge in the Berkeley Hills. Then the feds raided Ronnie's house and commandeered five cases of SKS rifles. But Ronnie performed a successful getaway into Mexico, vowing revenge on dad for ratting him out. It was a bona fide bummer. Ronnie had family in the AB—the Aryan Brotherhood—throughout the California prison system. They'd hunt for dad.

Superman hammered at me, "Your brother has a bomb. He's got it going on. And you? You ain't got jack shit.

What are you gonna do, peewee? You're getting old. Almost thirteen. The world won't wait for you to get it together. You'd better hurry up and do something or you'll be left behind."

Superman didn't divulge as to where I'd be left behind. Was it on the map? Kansas? Rhode Island? Two to one, you asked him what he meant, he'd hem and haw. Blah blah blah. But I had my own ideas. I'd be in limbo. Thirteen years old. Dead in the water.

I vamoosed from Superman's pad—too many things were on my mind, Frankie Jones among them. The ramshackle Glen Canyon cabin where the Crusade boy messed with her had been home to a group of Vietnam vets in the 1960s. The Lone Ranger's uncle, a vet himself, said the vets built campfires there—and they took acid to summon the spirits of their brethren who'd died in the war. In the days when Ronnie drove dad and me past the canyon to test weapons by San Bruno Mountain—scrawny urban deer grazed on the hillsides above the road—he never failed to point out the cabin to us. It was always blacked out.

TWENTY-THREE

A week later we got word from the police. Witnesses testified an elderly gentleman who could've been the old man was seen in Joshua Tree. Some people went to prison. Some went to Bakersfield. Others went to the desert.

I'd happened upon one other photograph of the old man. It was shot sometime in the 1950s. He was with a group of fellow railroad workers. There were three rows of them. All white men garbed in greasy overalls. The old man was in the second row, slightly apart from the others. His arms crossed over his chest. His eyes smoldering under a workingman's cap. His seamed face said: Show me something I don't already know.

The old man spoke broken English. Broken consonants. Broken vowels. I cringed with embarrassment every time he talked. The old lady—I'd hardly seen her since the old man left us—she was five times worse. She pulverized American words in her mouth until they were unrecognizable.

In Russia—in Odessa's ghetto streets—the old lady was called Serafina. Here in California, she had renamed herself Susan. With the old man gone, she'd never have to clip his toenails again. Boil cow's tongue with a pinch of salt for him. Or argue in Russian about the phone bill.

I reclined in my cot and brooded about the old man and the old lady. Mom blew into the bedroom, her slippered footfall muffled and soft on the linoleum floor. She lingered by the door, a Gorky paperback— *The Lower Depths*—tucked under her arm. "I must tell you something dreadful."

Her voice was a trap. I fell right into it. "What's that?"

She lit up the room with a self-conscious smile. "I have tuberculosis. Isn't it awful? I'm ashamed."

I went numb—something that was happening frequently as of late. Dad who was not my dad had TB—since he was eight years old. "Do you know who you got it from?"

"It wasn't your father. No, not him."

"Then who?"

"Another man. He wasn't very nice."

"You should've told me about this before now."

"Maybe. But it was better not to. I didn't want to worry you."

"You're so considerate."

"Yes, yes. I've always been like that. Looking out for others."

"Have you told Putin?"

"I haven't."

"Why not?"

"It's not necessary."

"Are you mental? How come?"

"He's a special child."

I was flummoxed. "Special? I don't get it."

"He won't catch TB."

"But I might?"

Her distant gray eyes swept over me. "You are not special."

I rendezvoused with Superman in the late afternoon—he and I legged it to Bernal Heights. From the hilltop we gave the city a once-over. Every neighborhood from the Marina to Visitacion Valley was drowning in smoke. The Financial District's buildings were buried under brown clouds of it. Superman nervously chattered about a guy at the clinic who'd had another kid iced for eight hundred and fifty bucks because the kid filched two thousand dollars of weed off him. "It's an omen, peewee. These are the last days. Get that through your little head."

I knew in my heart there was someplace better than this one. Somewhere, somewhere. A place where everyone had enough to eat. Where pickpockets and poets rubbed shoulders with kings and queens. A place where loneliness was simply a word in the dictionary. The promised land. Jerusalem.

But where was Jerusalem?

TWENTY-FOUR

The clock tick-tocked past midnight. Darkness found me under my blankets with dad's gun—the pistol smelled of his deodorant. I glared into the bedroom's murk. Putin stood by the window with his bomb, his sullen face otherworldly in the moonlight. I gave him the facts. "Mom says she has tuberculosis."

"That's a crock of shit," he scoffed. "She lies all the time."

"She said she didn't tell you about it."

"Why would she? It's pointless. I'll never get it."

"That's what she said."

"Because I'm the golden child."

"Yeah, right. Why don't you go to bed?"

"No way. I've been having a nightmare about dad."

"What about?"

Putin placed a hand on his bomb and absent-mindedly stroked it. "Him ripping off guns."

"What's the problem? He was born to do that."

"He wasn't happy with it."

"Jesus Christ. You sure of this? It's his bread and butter."

"He told me otherwise."

"Told you what?"

"In the nightmare he said he didn't want to do it because he was losing his touch."

"That's incredible. What else did he say?"

"Not much. He was too confused."

"Did he talk about Muscupiabe?"

"No, he didn't. It never came up."

"How about me?"

"He didn't mention you."

"Then what happened?"

"Nothing. It ended."

Putin's bad dream was my salvation. What a sap I'd been, taking responsibility for dad's arrest in Pacific Heights, never believing he'd engineered his own demise. Dad had disobeyed the most important commandment of a break-in: Don't stay in a mini-mansion longer than three minutes. He'd dawdled at the bathroom window with a pillowcase of guns. The sun in his face. The cops outside. Old dad. He'd gotten lost in the badlands.

□ □ □

What did Putin want from life? The very same thing everyone wanted—the right to live in peace. Yet his bomb pointed to a seldom-traveled road. A road only a few of us had the guts to walk on.

The golden child didn't let me touch his bomb. He wouldn't let anyone touch it. It was too delicate, he asserted. It had a hair-trigger mechanism—somebody who didn't know what they were doing might set it off. Also, there was no way to defuse the thing.

"Don't panic," he chided. "I've got it under control."

TWENTY-FIVE

Would I ever get to the promised land?

I found myself alone with Bob the social worker the morning after Putin told me about his dream. He and I sat in the front seat of his county sedan in our driveway.

The two of us studied mom through the sedan's mosquito-spattered windshield. She was on the stoop dunking her hair in a basin of peroxide—refreshing her bleach job. She lifted her head—a mop of yellowed locks whipped through the air before she captured it with a blue and red beach towel. It was straight out of *Doctor Zhivago* in California.

Bob cleared his throat. "I'll tell you why I'm here. I have news. But you won't like it. Did you know your dad got shanked in Muscupiabe this week?"

I breathed slowly. What a rush. "No, I didn't."

He pounded his fists on the steering wheel, and faked indignation—the poor boy didn't know his daddy was stabbed in prison. It was social worker theatrics. And I couldn't recall when I'd eaten last. Was it yesterday? I had acid reflux, cramps, a headache, tingling in my feet. Bob interrupted my train of thought. "You got plans to visit your dad?"

I weighed my response. "You'd have to ask mom."

"It might be a while. Getting shanked is a big deal. He was placed in protective custody for his own safety. Don't say I didn't tell you that. Now get out of here."

The almighty one had spoken. I threw open the passenger door and fell out of the car. Bob started up the sedan's engine, revved it, then he skidded from the driveway to the street. Going, going, gone. The prick.

Dad was in protective custody. Where informers were housed. My god. What a complete bringdown. Dad was shanked because he'd snitched on Ronnie. I couldn't whisper a thing about it to Putin. He was just a kid—it would crush him.

Mom was addicted to saying we were going to Muscupiabe to see dad. It would be a six-hour ride on a chartered bus. We'd have sun-charred Interstate Five for scenery, and convenience store sandwiches fortified with salmonella to snack on. The more she said we were going—an insane mantra—the clearer it became we wouldn't. In addition, mom refused to talk about the old man's departure to the desert. Her strategy: One part new world denial. One part old country stoicism. Two parts Prozac. Soundtrack by Stravinsky.

◻ ◻ ◻

Dusk. Horseflies and mosquitos trailed Putin and me as we advanced toward the Natoma checkpoint. I was tempted to tell him about dad, that he'd gotten shanked. To let Putin know two could play his game. I could hurt him like he'd hurt me. Putin thought dad was godlike. He learned dad was a snitch, that would spoil the picture. Fuck it up good. I should've done it. But I didn't. Lucky for Putin.

I didn't trust Putin—he was on an ego trip. He said he had his bomb under control. That was bogus. If anything, it controlled him. The way he roamed the streets with it—like a total zombie. A kid with a bomb? Who didn't know his ass from a hole in the ground? And him blustering he was going to blow up the world? There were times when I wished he would. But blowing up the world would require greater firepower than his weak-ass toy bomb.

Putin and I were a hundred feet shy of the checkpoint. Together we laid eyes on a bearded white man in a garbage bag poncho dozing on a slab of refrigerator cardboard. Two SWAT cops in blue jumpsuits and white helmets, a Mexican lady and a Black cat, were yelling at him to get to his feet. The lady cop prodded his leg with her baton and yawped he had to find somewhere else to sleep, or she'd radio in for an ambulance.

The man farted, then rotated onto his stomach. Putin inserted himself between him and the cops. "Mister, listen to what she's saying. You don't want no 5150."

The woman cop pointed her baton at Putin. "Shut your mouth. This ain't got fuck all to do with your ass."

Putin shrank from her. "You don't want to 5150 him."

"That's enough shit from you. He doesn't want to go to Napa State, then he can go to jail."

The guy sprang to his feet, and ran off with the cardboard. The cops then focused their attention on Putin. I didn't like the feel of it. Neither did Putin. In haste, he and I scattered. He jogged up Natoma. I trotted to Valencia Street and lost myself in the tourists that crowded the sidewalks.

□ □ □

Mom's TB was too much for me. Some days ago I'd happened upon a satchel in our hall closet. It bulged with black and white snapshots from mom's days as an artist's nude model—the times she was in between husbands. She'd posed in a bathtub. Sideways in front of a mirror. Stretched out on a bed. In one print her upturned face was a pool of light, a pool that waited for life—anyone's life—to be poured into it.

While we lived, angels guarded us. The dead—heavenly messengers—awaited us. Those were the rules.

I had to get a TB test.

TWENTY-SIX

Thursday I was at the clinic with the Lone Ranger. He said Superman was a newly minted Crusade for Jesus stool pigeon. The instructors had threatened Superman with arrest—they'd gotten the skinny about his liquor store job—if he didn't inform on the other kids. I'd recently overheard Superman chitchatting with Frankenstein before a Jesus session. Fraternizing with the enemy—a definite no-no.

The Lone Ranger's disclosure set the tone for the rest of the day. A riot had broken out at a charter school in the Sunset District. Crusade for Jesus boys had brawled with Black students bused over from Ingleside. A SWAT platoon rolled in and provided a buffet of tear gas, rubber bullets, and concussion grenades. The kids at the clinic couldn't stop talking about it. Everyone was jumpy. Our turn was coming.

□ □ □

For the second time in as many days Bob the social

worker called on us. Mom met him at our door in her finest halter top, a skimpy white vinyl thing with one functional strap. She also sported khaki shorts exhausted from years of battling to restrain her waist-line. They'd given up the fight and were defiantly unzipped.

Inside the apartment Bob camped on the living room couch with mom. At first, they didn't say anything to each other, wordlessly communing in the oldest language known to people—loneliness. Mom brushed a nonexistent fly off her knee. Bob picked his nose. The two of them then got down to brass tacks and pow-wowed about Putin and me. About what should be done with us. Bob and mom scrolled through the entire alphabet. It wasn't music. Detention. Electroshock therapy. Lockup. Napa State. Psychotropics. Putin loomed in the bedroom doorway with his bomb. "You shitbirds! I am the golden child! I'm going to blow up the world! You can't stop me!"

Okay. Today was one of those days I needed Putin to destroy the world. The sooner, the better. And it wasn't because mom and Bob the social worker were talking trash. But when the old man vanished into the desert, I'd lost my marbles. Not so long ago I was at his bun-galow to help him change his socks because he couldn't bend over and do it for himself. His grizzled head—redolent of horse radish and tobacco—was next to mine as I babbled, "Listen, old man, there's got to be something for me and Putin. We ain't getting enough to eat on welfare." He made a sour face like I was an idiot. At my age he'd toiled in a Donets Basin mine.

TWENTY-SEVEN

The week deepened, flies thickened, wasps multiplied, and the gulf between myself and the rest of the universe grew in leaps and bounds. New alliances were forming, old frontiers were crumbling. The Lone Ranger blathered to anyone who'd listen that Superman was a sellout. "Watch what you say around the motherfucker," the Lone Ranger advised.

I never told Superman that mom stole cigarettes and suppositories from the Walgreens on Divisadero Street. Or that Putin's specialty as a shoplifter was the Whole Foods store at Dolores and Market. Neither of them ever got busted. But the Lone Ranger was blowing it— he was arrested so frequently for stealing, he'd gotten straitjacketed to Napa State.

□ □ □

Early evening. The sky was the hue of week-old tomato juice. Mom threw together a supper of hot dogs, the kind sold for thirty-nine cents a package at the liquor store. As an extra treat, she baked biscuits with the weevil-infested government commodity flour she'd procured from welfare.

The meal was ready—the apartment fragrant with weevil flour. Putin, mom, and I huddled on the living room floor to dine. Paper plates and plastic forks. A genuine picnic. The hot dogs were leathery. The biscuits, like warm toilet paper.

"This is fucking nasty. I can't eat it."

I'd gone too far with my opinion. Mom's bone-white face went blank. Her nostrils flared dangerously—primed for another scene from *Doctor Zhivago* in California. "You no eat? I work hard to make it good! You no love your mother!"

Putin scrooched over his hot dog and cut it up into bite-sized chunks with a plastic knife.

He had his own movie—the nine-year-old bomber.

I jumped to my feet and bolted from the apartment.

□ □ □

I drifted by the welfare office on my walk. I recited a psalm for government commodities. For the unidentifiable canned meat—dog food was tastier. For the cheese suitable to plug holes in walls—it was indestructible. For the powdered eggs that got stuck in your teeth. For the corn syrup that guaranteed diabetes. For the weevil-infested white flour. For these were the days of my life.

I returned to a pitch-black apartment. The moon's crooked smile white against the shadow-blown windows. I snaked through the living room to the bedroom without disturbing mom. Putin sat up in his cot the second I was there. "I need to talk to you."

I held my breath until it hurt. "Can't it wait until tomorrow?"

"Nope."

My shoulders sagged in defeat. "Jesus. What is it?"

"I know what mom is doing."

"What do you mean?"

"Don't be thick. You know what the fuck I'm saying."

"Say I did, I wouldn't be asking."

"I'm talking about her creeping in here at night."

"Yeah?"

Putin sneezed, loud and wet. "I'm right there."

"Right where?"

"Here. Close enough to smell your fear. You're scared of her, aren't you?"

"I can't remember a day when I wasn't. She's nuts."

"Fuck that. She acts like a short eyes. Her and Bob the social worker. A short eyes controls your body. They take your spirit. You get under their thumb, you become a ghost. And Bob is Crusade for Jesus. He's trying to convert mom."

"How do you know that?"

Putin sneezed three times in a row. "I'm the golden child. I know everything. So what're you gonna do about it?"

"What can I do?"

"You have a pistol. That's a start."

"It's got nothing to do with you."

"All right then. Be that way. But now what?"

"I need to get out of this place."

"Where are you gonna go? You got options?"

"Jerusalem."

"And where is that, this Jerusalem of yours?"

"It's a billion miles away."

"Then you need something extra to get there."

"That's hocus-pocus."

Putin smirked at me. "It's not hocus-pocus. You have a faraway destination, you gotta invent something to get to it."

"Like what?"

"A device that will set you free. Like my bomb."

"But what about the old man?"

"What's he got to do with any of this?"

"Don't you worry about him?"

"No, I don't. Because wherever he's at, it's better than where we are."

The bomb was nestling in Putin's sheets.

A homemade toy. Itching to explode.

At ten o'clock the next morning the Mexicans staged a walkout at the clinic. The result of too many clashes with the security guards. Too many unanswered complaints about why the portraits of Jesus Christ plastered around the campus had the looks of a Crusade boy. The hallways were awash in kids streaming to the front gate. The guards attempted to hold them back—but everyone surged into Harrison Street, where they were welcomed by a double line of SWAT vans. A barrage of tear gas was fired; green-gray clouds of the crud wafted overhead. I located Putin—we'd walked with the Mexicans—and cut out.

◻ ◻ ◻

I spotted two messages on the answering machine at the apartment. One was from Bob the social worker. He prattled on about how he'd put in an appeal to expedite our food stamp application, confident there would be a happy ending. The other message was from the old lady. She spewed a cyclone of Russian and English, alternating between the two tongues before she hung up. I pressed the delete button.

I eavesdropped on mom two hours later—she was trilling in rapid-fire English on the phone: "You drove him away, ma! You know you did! He didn't disappear into the desert! You pushed him out! Don't tell me you didn't! That's a lie! You hate men! What? Of course, I hate men! And you know what, ma? You're killing me! You hear that? You're killing me!"

You didn't have to break and enter into houses in Jerusalem. Every door was open. You didn't have to steal. Everything was yours. Food stamps grew year-round on trees—you picked what you needed. Jerusalem, Jerusalem, I was coming to you.

TWENTY-EIGHT

Forty-eight hours passed without incident. Until mom related to me the old lady had gotten mugged on Market Street near the Civic Center BART station by two crackheads she'd befriended—a husband and wife team. They'd stolen her purse—which was ridiculous—because she stowed her money ghetto-style in her panties. But now the old lady was under observation at General Hospital.

I'd accompanied the old lady to the Safeway supermarket last Friday—her and the orthopedic shoes she'd worn since 1956. I watched as she quarreled with a cashier about the price of cauliflower. Mom said when the Nazis invaded Odessa the old lady had dodged bullets in the street. I couldn't put together the child that evaded the Nazis with the ancient woman losing her composure in the supermarket. She petrified me, how her brown eyes glimmered with pleasure whenever she was angry.

I was so much like her, it wasn't funny.

In my prime, during my halcyon days—I was five

years old—the old lady schooled me on how to snoop through a house without anyone knowing it. What the Nazis taught her in the old world—a silent child was the child that survived—served me well in the new world. The gun thief that was quieter than a graveyard was a thief who stayed out of jail.

After the news about the old lady, I sauntered to Whole Foods to lift some toothpaste—it was that or brush my teeth with bar soap. I collided into the Lone Ranger at the corner of Fifteenth and Mission. Out of breath—he had asthma and wheezed—the Lone Ranger regaled me with the latest news. Lackner the undercover had waylaid him on Lexington Street. "That fucking cop makes me antsy. He talked out of the side of his neck, asking me whether Superman did the liquor store. I didn't say nothing to Lackner. Not a damn word."

The Lone Ranger never wore his mask.

And me? I was ready to take a rocket ship into outer space.

◻ ◻ ◻

Twilight. Bands of purpling sunlight filtered into the bedroom window. Mom sobbed in the living room—her cries seeped through the paper-thin walls. "Papa, please help me. I'm going meshugga. Help me, papa. I can't go on."

Depression had drawn mom into a pit so deep—Prozac or no Prozac—there wasn't any way to get out of it. Nobody was going to come and help her. Not Bob the social worker. None of her husbands. Not her mother. Fucking no one. Especially the old man—she didn't even know where he was.

I was nodding off as they surrounded me in the near-dark. Frankie Jones. The Crusade boys. Lackner the undercover. Bob the social worker. Partisans with frostbitten feet. Dad wielding a Mossberg shotgun—looking very pleased with himself.

"Get away from me," I pleaded. "I've had enough."

Putin fluffed his pillow, and groused, "Who you talking to?"

"No one," I softly replied. "No one at all."

TWENTY-NINE

Life's inner secrets were revealed to me the morning dad got jailed on a firearms charge by SWAT—an unloaded pistol in the trunk of his car. It was a few months before his initial stretch in Muscupiabe. Mom and I visited the cop shop to check on his status. Could we post bond?

At the police station we palavered with the desk sergeant—he sat behind a bulletproof glass window. I was convinced he was god with his unsmiling white visage, gray hair, blue uniform, and silver buttons. A god who had power, not only over dad, but me too. A god that would show no mercy should I have the nerve to step out of line. Should I defy him. A god who understood I didn't belong here. Not in his crummy world. At any rate, dad's gun charge was thrown out of court—illegal search and seizure.

◻ ◻ ◻

The day after mom called out to the old man for help, I intercepted her staggering in the kitchenette with her bathrobe undone. She steadied herself against the counter, her face waxy from Prozac and sleeplessness. A moment went by before she figured out who I was. She rasped at me, "You smell bad."

I had to get away from mom—I booked over to Superman and Tony's place. Like this was a good idea or something. I was at their door, right as Tony propelled Superman through it. Tony followed Superman onto the stoop and slugged him three times. Kapow— Superman went down on both knees.

"Fuck you, Superman! I'm positive!"

I was hypnotized by Tony's anger, the way it electrified the air, and how it made my head spin. No less hypnotic was Superman's mug—his weary eyes were far, far away.

Earth to Superman. Earth to Superman.

What galaxy were you from?

I snuffled my armpits—they didn't smell so bad.

□ □ □

Lackner the undercover pushed on with the manhunt for the liquor store robber. The police had informed the public an unidentified male approached a Brink's truck in the store's parking lot last December. He'd brandished a burner at two Brink's employees. The victims mistook the cell phone for a gun and handed over everything in the truck. The perp fled south on Mission Street with a sack of money.

The loot showed up at a homeless camp under the freeway near Otis Street. At a garbage dumpster in Franklin Square frequented by recyclers, and at a soup kitchen on the outskirts of Mission Bay. The canvas bag that contained the cash was recovered from the shores of Stow Lake in Golden Gate Park—it'd been doused with bleach to hinder forensics.

Superman had been philosophical about the circumstances. "The cops will never find no one. They don't even know who they're searching for. And the paper was going to the bank. So it went the other direction. To the sufferers in the street. Ain't that good news?"

Whatever Superman's faults were—they were myriad, stamping him with the most screwed-up personality in the solar system—his generosity had thrilled me. He was just like Frankie Jones. What they stole, they gave to other people. Wasn't this the core of crime itself? The very definition of it? To enrich the less fortunate? I was saddened dad hadn't been like that. The schmuck wouldn't be in Muscupiabe had he been that smart. It was a lesson to cherish: You never stole anything for yourself. You only thieved to help others.

THIRTY

Wednesday morning I repaired to the medical clinic in the parking lot at Sixteenth and Bryant. I told the doctor there I needed a tuberculosis test. He made several phone calls and obtained an appointment for me to visit one of his colleagues in the afternoon. A hotshot pediatric specialist considered the best in the city. I got uneasy. What would someone in that position want to do with me?

One o'clock. Fighting off the feeling it was a mistake, I set out to the specialist's office—his place of business was in a Victorian mansion on California Street. A block away from it, I paused in an alley to take a leak—I drained myself on a palm tree's trunk. While I peed, I succumbed to the reverie which often occurred at such moments. I woolgathered about Jerusalem—for sure I'd get a birthday cake there.

A nurse had me fill out insurance forms in the doctor's office, then I was escorted into an air-conditioned examining room. I sat in a chair and fingered my electronic bracelet. The pediatrician, an unmasked tanned white man, came in moments later. I muttered to myself, fuck, I should've known his name.

The dirtbag that messed with Frankie Jones?

The doctor was his father.

I couldn't believe my luck. And so I did what I always did when I was cowed and someone like him had the clout to help me and I already knew he wouldn't—I smiled. My stomach growled with hunger. Somebody with money was about to push me down. I smiled as he grated, "I'm sorry, but I talked to my nurse about your problem and I'm puzzled why you were sent to us. We don't accept welfare cases."

Thanks, mister. Have a nice day.

I skedaddled from the pediatrician's office, frazzled by the misadventure with him. I was on Bush Street and I got a noseful of boiled cow's tongue off a zephyr blowing in from the East Bay. It was the old man reaching out to me. Boiled cow's tongue. Who else could it be?

The old lady had a vision during her stay at General Hospital—the old man in the afterlife. He was waiting for her at the end of a tunnel of white light. That's the underworld, she'd marveled. It had terrified her, she told mom. She couldn't escape her husband. Hadn't she given him seventy years of her mortal existence—wasn't this sufficient? Or must she spend the hereafter with him too?

What did angels say?

God only knew. They'd never consulted my family.

◻ ◻ ◻

During our final months of doing jobs together, dad and I proceeded to break into a series of mini-mansions near the Presidio. The last job was in a cul-de-sac by Alta Plaza. It was a victorious undertaking. Dad was ecstatic at having nabbed a brace of handguns. Colt .45 pistols with mother-of-pearl grips.

We were living the American dream.

I thought those days would never end.

But they did.

The good life petered out on Christmas Day—after dad said I'd get my own gun rack. Putin, mom, and I motored with him to Half Moon Bay in San Mateo County to spend the holiday at the seashore.

It was a mild December day. The sun at the beach kissed our faces while an offshore wind flogged our legs. Mom flaunted a white terry cloth bikini. Dad was in threadbare red Speedos which highlighted his potbelly. Putin and I frolicked in the surf, and played tag with the jellyfish. Dad dropped a bombshell on us—we were in Half Moon Bay to hook up with one of his old cellmates from Muscupiabe. What dad neglected to bring up—which I heard later—it was a cat named Jack he had a yen for.

We got to Jack's house—a beachfront condo gone to seed. It dawned on dad the relationship with his former cellie had shifted. Jack was a blond, meek guy shacked up with a Mexican woman and her two kids. The revelation gave rise to a foul mood in dad. He and Jack exchanged hurtful words. We evacuated Half Moon Bay under a black cloud.

The drive up the coastline to the city was tense—dad was fuming over Jack. That was when I began to see a pattern in dad—his knack for misreading situations. But mom didn't misread them. Her marriage to dad unraveled after the New Year and soon thereafter they ceased sleeping in the same bed. For the remainder of winter and the spring that flirted behind it, he and I adhered to our regular schedule of breaking and entering mini-mansions. Until we broke into the wrong one. Flat-out busted.

I had to give dad credit where it was due. His fantasies— how he'd yearned for Jack—were central to an underground man like himself. In the no man's land where dad dwelled, far away from common sense and sanity, truths and lies were meaningless. Take it from me. Nothing was real.

◻ ◻ ◻

That's how it was. For months I'd been living in a dreamworld. Days running from the cops when a job went awry. Hours spent on my knees in the prayer room. I wanted to slow down, but I'd never learned how.

And now it was too late.

THIRTY-ONE

A fortnight after the old lady was discharged from the hospital, the smoke lifted and the stars and the moon sparkled as Putin and I trolled up the driveway to the garage apartment. The front door was ajar—we made our way into the living room. It would've been better if we hadn't. A punk-ass high school kid, someone we didn't know, was fucking mom on the couch. The kid's jeans were bunched at his ankles, the globes of his spotty butt clenched tight. He checked out Putin and me. Still in the saddle, he deduced we were a pair of harmless runts. "What do you dweebs want here? I'm busy."

Mom refused to look at Putin or me.

The kid bargained with us. "I'll lay some herb on you guys. Just let me have a few minutes to finish up. What do you say?"

Putin gave him a stiff middle finger.

My brother and I ducked out of the apartment.

We tromped up Mission Street to Superman and Tony's crib. Our shoes clacked on the garbage-strewn pavement, the police-bright streetlights washed us in circles of hot yellow-white light. The street was so quiet, we could hear the electricity in the power lines above our heads.

I ached to tell Putin that mom had done her best to keep it together. She was the daughter of a miner from Kiev and a woman from Odessa. From a country steeped in bloodshed, famine, and war. Her soul was haunted by the motherland.

History was another short eyes.

We were its hostages.

I never blamed mom for anything she did—sometimes.

She'd always said: "I wasn't meant to be a mother or wife."

What Putin and I had just seen in our living room?

Mom wasn't kidding.

Tony and Superman were in the kitchen at their apartment when Putin and I came through. We squeezed into the narrow room with them—the walls began to sweat from our body heat.

Superman wanted us to go for a ride with him and Tony. A cruise to celebrate summer. I didn't know what he was talking about. As far as I was concerned—the fucking virus—summer couldn't end soon enough. Everyone was jittery, talking through their masks. Tony's eyes were feverish, glassy with exhaustion. Superman flourished his car keys, yelping in his squeaky voice. Putin winked, and thumbed his nose at me. For a moment, I didn't mind that Tony was positive, or that Superman was a Crusade for Jesus stool pigeon, or if Putin hated my guts.

I just didn't care.

Because nobody talked English better than me.

We left the apartment, piled into Superman's whip, and got going, churning up Mission Street. With Putin beside me in the back seat, I glued my nose to the window. I regarded the palm trees, those that were alive, the streetlights whizzing by, and the shabby linoleum and stucco buildings in neat little rows with everybody cozy and safe inside them. I didn't ask for anything in this life, I'd be safe too. That was what I wanted. To be safe. For once.

THIRTY-TWO

It would have been smarter had we gone to Bakersfield with Frankie Jones. I still had my nose glued to the window when we hung a right onto Market Street. A SWAT cruiser zeroed in on us from behind—its blue and red lights flooded the Malibu's interior. Superman had a gander in his rearview and chortled, "What the hell. It's no big deal."

Superman pulled over for the cops by the Zuni Café—before he could ask them what the problem was, four SWAT tac guys in body armor exploded from the cruiser and overran the Malibu. They pried open the doors and smashed the windows with their shotguns—Superman was seized by his hair and dragged out of the driver's seat, then heaved onto the pavement. He struggled to his feet, only to get tasered—a quivering taser prong jutted from his neck as he capsized to the ground. Another cop pepper sprayed Tony in the eyes, leaving him spluttering, "You scumbags! I'm positive!"

A cop reached in the car, grabbed me by the throat, and choked me out. "You're dead, you little bitch." I was dumped on the curb—handcuffed for the third time that summer.

I regained consciousness in time to get a glimpse of Putin. He was the last one in the Malibu. I wanted to yell at him that we would eat good soon. Lasagna and pizza and strawberry ice cream and macaroon cookies. The works. Then we'd go to the desert to find the old man. And then he and I would take the bus to visit dad, who wasn't my dad but his dad, at Muscupiabe.

Putin acted like he'd known this was coming. Taking it slow, he squirmed out of the car—until the cops caught on to his bomb. "He's got a bomb! The asshole has a bomb!"

The Russian boy with summer glowing in his eyes.

The golden child.

Destined for greatness.

Standing on the verge of blowing up the world.

In Putin's eyes I saw the letter mom received from the warden's office at Muscupiabe. It said dad had been shanked again—post his release from protective custody. Then in rapid succession I saw the old man in the Russian snow hunting Nazis with a knife between his teeth. Frankie Jones in a shadowy room waiting for someone to comfort her. The Crusade boy who got her pregnant at a Union Street restaurant with his new girl-friend. I saw the roofs of Jerusalem—they shimmered on the horizon.

Putin stepped away from the Malibu—the styrofoam blocks in his phony bomb tumbled out of mom's black babushka stockings. His eyes met mine in that instant. Some people went to prison. Some went to Bakersfield. Others went to the desert.

The cops opened fire on Putin—a dozen bullets sizzled toward him. The shots pushed him one way, then another—his neck snapped to and fro; he danced and danced until he couldn't dance. He collapsed in a heap under a flickering streetlight, his chest riddled with holes, his blood pooling into the gutter, his gaze—the gaze of a martyr—trained on me.

PART THREE

BEHIND THE IRON CURTAIN

THIRTY-THREE

Frankie Jones had the baby by herself at a hospital in Bakersfield. A nurse asked her, "You got someone with you, sweetie?" She said, "No, nobody." The nurse tapped Frankie's wrist, and eyed her with bloodshot peepers that had seen a million births and deaths.

"Don't worry, honey, we'll take good care of you."

Frankie endured twenty-one hours in labor, and delivered a seven-pound boy. The nurse placed the newborn infant in her arms—Frankie felt his heat, sniffed the thatch of his black hair, and feasted her eyes on his face. Her face. What she'd told the baby's daddy's mother was as right as her child was fatherless—the world had become a different place.

Frankie didn't name her son. A name would come. But not yet. She had to wait. For the right one, for something honest. A name he could call his own. A name to be a passport to his future.

She stayed another month at her aunt and uncle's. They were not overjoyed at having Frankie and the baby in their small house, though they never came right out and said it, too uptight to bare what was on their minds. Frankie told them she was departing—they didn't stop her.

Frankie packed up the baby's things and walked down to the bus station with her infant. Right before she crossed the threshold into it, the birds perched on the nearby telephone lines cheeped: Frankie Jones, Frankie Jones, Frankie Jones. Where will you go?

She'd go where her baby could get a start.

Frankie donned her mask.

The birds went on with their singing.

Frankie bought a one-way bus ticket in the station. The ticket seller wrinkled his nose at her son, and grunted, "Cute kid. He cry a lot?" Frankie said her baby was tranquil in a way most things in life weren't.

She boarded a coach, and found a seat midway between the front and the toilet at the rear. She laid her son against a milk-swollen breast, and lulled him to sleep by jiggling her knee.

THIRTY-FOUR

I had the strangest vibe about Frankie Jones that morning, like something had happened to her, a sensation which left me dizzy and wrung out. I shook off the feeling and watched Putin navigate his motorized wheelchair through the garage apartment. He piloted the chair into the kitchenette—scraping the paint off its walls. It was the latest development in a weeks-long journey that began on a summer night at General Hospital when the surgeons dug three police slugs out of him during an emergency operation.

The bullets were extracted from Putin, but their evil stayed with him. Oftentimes—if he thought no one was within earshot—he sat in his wheelchair and ranted at the walls in our bedroom. He'd been halfway to heaven after the surgery—closer to death than life—before the devil snatched him from god's arms, and hurled his ass back to earth.

Some doctors said Putin would walk again.

More said he wouldn't.

The district attorney's office justified Putin's shooting by saying an APB had been issued shortly before the deed—a primer-gray vehicle similar to Superman's whip was identified in the vicinity of an armed robbery on Nob Hill. A grand jury was convened to delve into the affair—but it disbanded after coming up with zilch. So the old lady and mom filed a lawsuit against the city—their lawyer was gunning for an out-of-court settlement.

Nowadays SWAT patrol cars boated past the garage apartment. They aimed spotlights at our door and called us out by name on their loudspeakers to let us know they had not forgotten Putin. The ocean wind rattled against our windows to say it hadn't forgotten him either.

Superman did thirty days in county jail—collateral damage from the shooting. Last week his throat was slashed at a shebang in the Excelsior that went haywire. He was recovering from the knifing at his auntie's house in Antioch.

I didn't know where Tony was.

Perhaps up north. Chico. Fort Bragg. Santa Rosa. Wherever it was more peaceful than the city—should there be places like that anymore.

Four days ago we got a message from the Lone Ranger.

He said it was a drag what Putin had been put through. He also relayed a rumor to us. Frankie Jones had taken the bus to Oklahoma to live with her folks. And himself? Well, the Lone Ranger was in Napa State—busted for shoplifting again.

Frankie Jones, the Lone Ranger, Superman, and Tony were out of my life. Probably for good. As I recalled what we shared, what we'd done together, my memory got fuzzy. I didn't remember my friends—what I remembered now were the voices in my head.

I'd read aloud to Putin throughout his brief stay at a welfare convalescent home in the Richmond District. Novels by Lermontov and Solzhenitsyn. Anna Akhmatova and Osip Mandelstam's poetry. *The Rise and Fall of the Third Reich*—including the footnotes. We heard from the cops that the old man had been sighted in Palm Springs. We also heard from dad's lawyer. Dad was back in protective custody—Ronnie's people in the Aryan Brotherhood were still hot on his trail. The war between Russia and Ukraine didn't make things any prettier. Crusade boys had spray-painted the garage apartment: PUTIN GO HOME.

The good news was the clinic's contract with the Division of Juvenile Justice had been canceled—fallout from the wildcat walkout by the Mexican kids. The campus on Harrison Street was permanently shuttered.

◻ ◻ ◻

Dear dad. The day after he and I got popped in Pacific Heights, I was towed into the downtown ATF office for an interview. The cops wanted to know why the guns confiscated from dad's car had their serial numbers erased. How often I'd seen dad file off the numbers from an AR-15 assault rifle snug in a vise grip. His finger stumps working at the gun metal. A self-satisfied grin on his sweaty, unshaven face. I didn't tell the cops a thing.

Mom was peeved at me for shielding dad. A man who slept with men. A man who slept with women too. A man happiest tinkering with his Thompson submachine gun. It had been forever since I was with him—he'd become another echo in my mind.

THIRTY-FIVE

At midday—mom and the old lady were getting commodities at welfare—I helped Putin maneuver his wheelchair out the screen door. He hurtled down the recently installed plywood ramp to the driveway. The crows in the neighbor's avocado tree cawed as he jockeyed his chariot to the street and braked it at the curb. I joined him there—a swarm of orange-brown dragonflies haloed our heads. Gingerly, I probed my brother. "How are you feeling?"

His blood-flecked eyes—sunken a mile into his skull—savaged me. "Don't be a dick. You know how I'm doing."

I feinted and parried. "I'm just asking about your health."

"Spare me the saccharin."

"What the hell is wrong with you, man?"

"You're what's wrong. Let's change the topic, shall we?" Putin sucked in a breath and leaned forward in the wheelchair. He scrutinized me and searched for a weak spot—he didn't have to search too hard. "Mom says you're campaigning again for a birthday cake."

I was taken aback. Putin was going for my jugular vein. The beast. I bristled: "Yeah, I am."

"But you've never had a cake before."

"No, I haven't."

"What makes you think you'll ever have one?"

"Is there something you're not telling me?"

"The obvious, you dolt. You won't get a cake."

"But you do. Big ones. Creamy and chocolate. You even let me have teeny-weeny slices."

"I'm generous."

"C'mon, why don't you help me?"

"You mean talk to mom? About getting you a cake?"

"Can you do it? Please?"

He noted the eagerness in my face. How I was willing to throw myself at his mercy. I'd let him lord it over me. I would grovel and kiss his feet. Putin reacted to my modest request with a heartwarming smile. "Absolutely not. Forget it."

I smiled too. I'd gotten what I expected—bupkis. While I digested that bitter nugget, Putin pointed a finger at the street. "Whoa, check this out."

He did that a lot since he'd gotten out of the convalescent home—he changed subjects and shifted gears at the drop of a hat. Oh, how he blabbed whatever he thought with no concern for anybody else. I rarely listened to the golden child these days.

Disgruntled, I scowled at what Putin was pointing at.

Then I shut my eyes.

Should the world close in on you—sorrow blotting out the light in your life—that light had to go somewhere. The little white boy in the supermarket had asked, "Did you find any treasures?" In a city where dogs with soft, defeated eyes got thrown from cars, where food stamps never arrived, nobody told me about this.

I opened my eyes and watched a young masked woman with a baby in a sling float past the SWAT checkpoint on Mission Street. A summery green chiffon dress clung to her slim frame. Her skin was the palest brown possible, as if she hadn't had a lick of sunshine in months.

The woman made a beeline—she had radar—to Putin's wheelchair and stopped in front of it. Without ceremony, she pulled her kid from the sling and plopped it in Putin's lap, then stepped back. The pink-cheeked infant looked up at my brother and gurgled with merriment.

I wanted to scream and scream and scream.

Oklahoma, my ass.

Frankie Jones was here—inches from me.

I couldn't take my eyes off her. The chiseled face that drove Crusade boys to their knees. The brains which made well-heeled Crusade girls ill with envy. The fingers that were deft enough to pick any sucker's pocket. Frankie Jones cocked a hip and removed her mask. She addressed Putin. "Do you know who I am?"

Putin flushed and bowed his head. "I sure do."

She gaped at him. "Let me ask you something. You mind? No? It was you outside my window, wasn't it?"

He didn't hesitate. "Yeah, that was me."

"Christ, what a life." Frankie raised her eyes skyward, took in the brown clouds, then she gazed at Putin. "You were there praying for me, weren't you?"

"I was."

"Why did you do that? You didn't have to."

To my astonishment, Putin began to weep; huge teardrops poured down his cheeks. I was stunned by his emotion, but even more so by his flawless English—the merest trace of an accent. "Your deportation, it was fucked up. It hurt me royally."

"That was Pluto."

"What was?"

"Bakersfield. But do you believe in god?"

Putin wiped his tears with the back of his left hand, his right hand too crippled from the police shooting to do anything. "Hell, no. Look at the mess I'm in."

"Who did you pray to then?"

His anguished blue eyes burned into her. "Mother Russia."

"Tell me your name." Frankie touched his shoulder.

The baby wriggled in Putin's arms. Red-faced, he mumbled, "Vladimir."

She repeated his name to herself. She chewed the syllables in her perfect mouth. Lingered over them. Tasted them. Weighed them. I was dying to let her know it was Mayakovsky's first name. That he stood for liberty. That he'd write poems about her. For the new world.

I bit my lip—it wasn't up to me to say any of that.

Frankie Jones stared harder at Putin. She whispered to the golden child, "That's what's up. Vladimir. Okay. I want to name my child after you."

"Holy shit," he gasped, "are you fucking kidding me?"

She was whispering, almost inaudible. "No, I'm not. Do I have your permission? I want it."

Putin's face grew redder. "You have my permission."

"Then this is how we do it." Frankie held out her arms to him. "This is where it starts. You've given me a gift, little man."

Everything quieted around them.

Flies didn't buzz. Mosquitos didn't hum.

Shadows didn't move.

I listened to the spaces between Frankie and Putin's words—the silences where the power of poetry resided—the spaces where freedom was. I didn't know how it could last, the freedom, but it was there, and it was ours.

Time could've stopped here—I would have been happy if it had. Frankie stooped and planted a kiss on Putin's forehead, her lipstick leaving a glossy red smudge on his brow. She plucked her baby from his wheelchair and piped, "I have to go. I've got business on the other side of the tracks. But I'll be back soon."

Putin's eyes were half-closed—drunk on Frankie's kiss. He was still weeping. "You promise?"

Before I got it through my head it wasn't a mirage, like one of those hallucinations mom had if she didn't take her pills, Frankie Jones put the kid in its sling, and she strode north on Mission Street. Her green dress incandescent in the black smoked-out sunlight as she left behind the SWAT checkpoint.

I didn't know where Frankie was going. Maybe up the hill to Pacific Heights. The neighborhood where there was no linoleum or stucco, where you could almost forget people died. To tell her baby's daddy his son had a name. A poet's name.

Some people went to prison.

Others went to the desert.

Some went to Bakersfield, and came back.

◻ ◻ ◻

The sun was hoisting its molten head over the smoke on Twin Peaks when I left Putin and started after Frankie. I edged past the checkpoint and the bus stop where a bunch of Crusade for Jesus leaflets gathered dust, and I moved right on by the liquor store Superman robbed in December. I had to see Frankie one more time, I had to—the woman Mayakovsky could've loved—for she knew life's inner secrets, and I was only beginning to comprehend them.

I walked south of Market while a breeze gusted in from the ocean with the scent of brine, clean and pure, and for a split second, I was young again. Nothing was broken, the slate was unblemished. No voices ricocheted in my head. Tomorrow belonged to me. I called out, "Frankie! Frankie! Wait up! I'm coming with you!"

But I was dreaming. Frankie Jones and her kid were long gone, and I was walking by myself, walking through the badlands.